The Case of the
Mischievous Doll

Also Available in Large Print
by Erle Stanley Gardner:

The Case of the Postponed Murder ✓
The Case of the Ice-Cold Hands

Erle Stanley Gardner

The Case of the Mischievous Doll

G.K. HALL & CO.
Boston, Massachusetts
1981

Library of Congress Cataloging in Publication Data

Gardner, Erle Stanley, 1889-1970.
  The case of the mischievous doll.

Large print ed.
1. Large type books. I. Title.
[PS3513.A6322M5 1981]   813'.52   80-29296
ISBN 0-8161-3215-1

An abridged version of this novel was published in
The Saturday Evening Post in 1962.

Published in Large Print by arrangement with William
Morrow and Company

Set in Penta / Mergenthaler Linotron 202 18 pt Times Roman

Foreword

As a rule the experts in legal medicine come from the medical profession. Many of them are both doctors of medicine and lawyers.

Others, however, have specialized in the law and then because of interest in the medical aspects of the legal profession have become medicolegal specialists.

The point is that the area where law and medicine overlap is a field of vital importance to the public, and yet, one which is little understood by the public.

My friend, W. R. Rule, Major, USAF, MSC, started out in the field of law, then specialized in the field of legal medicine, particularly as it applies to the military.

Having studied law in this country as

well as in England, Major Rule is currently the Legal Counsel for the Armed Forces Institute of Pathology, and has occupied that position since early 1959.

From time to time in connection with his official activities I have corresponded with him and have been impressed by the man's zeal, his clear-cut understanding of the importance of legal medicine, his high sense of duty, and his feeling that there has been too much separation of law, medicine and law enforcement, and that these sciences should be more closely connected and better understood.

Despite the fact that relatively few people realize it, the Armed Forces have developed nearly as perfect a system for the administration of justice as human minds can devise; and because this is true, they are taking a keen and ever-increasing interest in the field of legal medicine, particularly in co-ordinating forensic pathology with their investigations.

There are several outstanding

individuals in this field, and from time to time, with their permission, I intend to dedicate books to them, calling to the attention of the public the work these men are doing and the importance of that work.

Because Major W. R. Rule has such a clear concept of the importance of legal medicine in the administration of justice and has done so much to improve the administration of justice in and through the military, I dedicate this book to my friend,

W. R. RULE, Major, USAF, MSC, Legal Counsel, AFIP.

Erle Stanley Gardner

Chapter One

Della Street, Perry Mason's confidential secretary, entering Mason's private office, approached the big desk where the lawyer was seated and said, "A law office is the *darnedest* place."

"It certainly is," Mason said. "Now may I ask what brings forth this observation?"

"A certain Miss Dorrie Ambler."

"And I take it Miss Ambler is in the outer office, asking for an appointment?"

"She says she has to see you *right* away."

"How old?"

"Twenty-three or -four, but she's been around."

"Description?"

"Auburn hair, hazel eyes, five feet three; around a hundred and twelve; figure, thirty-four, twenty-four, thirty-four."

"And now," Mason said, "we come to the comment of yours — a law office is the *darnedest* place. What brought that up?."

"You could guess for a long time," she said, "but you would never guess what Miss Ambler wants — that is, at least what she says she wants."

"I'll bite," Mason said. "What does she want?"

"She wants to show you her operation," Della Street said.

"Her *what?*"

"Her operation."

"A malpractice suit, Della?"

"Apparently not. She seems to feel that there is going to be some question as to her identity and she wants to prove to you who she is, or rather, who she is not. She wishes to do this by showing you the scar of an appendectomy."

"What is this," Mason asked, "a gag? Or is she laying the foundation for

2

some sort of a shakedown? I certainly am not going to permit any young woman to walk in here and —''

''She wants witnesses present,'' Della Street said.

Mason grinned. ''Now *this* would be right down Paul Drake's alley. . . .I take it her figure is one that he would appreciate.''

''Leave it to Paul,'' she said. ''He has a keen eye. . . .Shall I call him?''

''Let's talk with our client first,'' Mason said. ''I am anxious to see the mysterious Miss Ambler.''

''Before I bring her in,'' Della Street said, ''there is one other thing you should know.''

Mason said, ''Della, I get very, very suspicious when you start breaking things to me in easy stages. Now, suppose you tell me the whole story *now*.''

''Well,'' Della Street said, ''your prospective client is carrying a gun in her purse.''

''How do you know?'' Mason asked.

''I don't actually know,'' Della Street

said. "I am quoting Gertie."

"Gertie," Mason said, grinning, "sits there at the switchboard, sizes up clients as they come in, and works her imagination overtime. And she has a very high-powered imagination."

"Conceded," Della Street said, "but Miss Ambler put her purse on that plastic-covered seat in the outer office and, as she leaned forward to get a magazine, touched the purse with her elbow — that plastic is a slippery as a cake of wet soap. The purse dropped to the floor and when it hit it made a heavy thud.

"Gertie says that Miss Ambler jumped about a foot, and then looked around guiltily to see if anyone had heard the sound of the heavy object striking the floor."

"Did Gertie let on?" Mason asked.

"Not Gertie," Della Street said. "You know how Gertie is. She has eyes all over her body but she keeps a poker face and you never know just what she's seen. However, Gertie has an imagination that can take a button, sew a

4

vest on it and then not only give you a description of the pattern of the vest, but tell you exactly what's in the pockets — and the stuff that's in the pockets is always connected with some romantic drama of Gertie's own particular type of thinking.''

"And in this case?" Mason asked.

"Oh, in this case," Della Street said, "Dorrie Ambler is an innocent young girl who came to the big city. She has been betrayed by a big, bad monster of a wolf who is now leaving the girl in a strange city to fend for herself. And Dorrie had decided to confront him with his perfidy and a gun. He will have the horrible alternative of making an honest woman out of her or being the *pièce de résistance* at Forest Lawn.''

Mason shook his head. "Gertie should be able to do better than that," he said.

"Oh, but Gertie has. She has already created the man in the case and clothed him with a whole series of ideas that are very typically Gertie. The man in the case, in case you're interested, is the son of a very wealthy manufacturer. The father has picked out a woman that he wants the boy to marry. The boy is really in love with Dorrie Ambler, but he doesn't want to disobey his father, and the father, of course, is going to disinherit the boy in the event he marries Dorrie. The boy is a nice enough kid, in a way, but rather weak."

"And what about Dorrie?" Mason asked.

"Oh, Dorrie, according to Gertie's scenario, is a very determined young woman who has a mind of her own and isn't going to let the father dominate her life or ruin her happiness."

"Hardly the type of innocent young woman who would permit herself to be seduced by a young man who has no particular force of character," Mason said.

"You'll have to argue with Gertie about that," Della Street told him. "Gertie's got the whole script all finished in her mind and no one's going to change it. When Gertie gets an idea in her head, it's there.

"You could pound dynamite in her

6

ear, set off the charge and blow most of her head away, but the idea would still remain intact.''

''Well,'' Mason said, ''I guess under the circumstances, Della, we'll have to see Dorrie Ambler and find out how Gertie's romantic mind has magnified the molehill into the mountain.''

''Don't sell Dorrie short,'' Della Street warned. ''She's a mighty interesting individual. She looks like a quiet, retiring young woman but she knows her way around and she wasn't born yesterday.''

Mason nodded. ''Let's have a look at her, Della.''

Della slipped through the door to the outer office and a few moments later returned with Dorrie Ambler in tow.

''So nice of you to see me, Mr. Mason,'' Dorrie Ambler said in a rapid-fire voice.

''You are concerned about a problem of personal identification?'' Mason asked.

''Yes.'

''And you wanted to have me take

7

steps to . . . well, let us say, to be sure you are you?''

"Yes."

"Why are you so anxious to establish your individual indentification?" Mason asked.

"Because I think an attempt is going to be made to confuse me with someone else.''

"Under those circumstances," Mason said, glancing at Della Street, "the very best thing to do would be to take your fingerprints.''

"Oh, but *that* wouldn't do at all!''

"Why not?"

"It would make me — well, make a criminal out of me.''

Mason shook his head. "You can have your fingerprints taken and send them to the FBI to be put in their non-criminal file. Actually every citizen should do it. It establishes an absolute means of identification.''

"How long does it take?''

"To have the fingerprints taken and sent on? Only a very short time.''

"I'm afraid I don't have that much

time, Mr. Mason. I want you to — well, I want to establish my identity with *you*. I want you to look me over, to . . ." She lowered her eyes, ". . . to see the scar of an operation."

Mason exchanged a quizzical glance with Della Street.

"Perhaps," Mason said, "you'd better tell me just what you have in mind, Miss Ambler."

"Well," she said demurely, "you'd know me if you saw me again, wouldn't you?"

"I think so," Mason said.

"And your secretary, Miss Street?"

"Yes," Della Street said. "I'd know you."

"But," she said, "people want to be absolutely certain in a situation of this sort and — Well, when the question of identification comes up they look for scars and . . . well, I have a scar."

"And you want to show it to us."

"Yes."

"I believe my secretary told me that you'd like to have some other witness present."

"Yes, as I understand it, a lawyer can't be a witness for his client."

"He shouldn't be," Mason said.

"Then perhaps we can get someone who could be a witness."

"There's Paul Drake," Mason said, again glancing at Della Street. "He's head of the Drake Detective Agency. He has offices on this floor and does most of my work."

"I would have preferred a woman," she said. "It's — rather intimate."

"Of course," Mason said, "you could retire to one of the other rooms and Della Street could make an inspection."

"No, no," she said hastily. "I want *you* to see, personally."

Mason glanced at Della Street again and said, "I'll send a message to Paul Drake. We'll see if we can get him to step in for a few minutes."

The lawyer pulled a pad of paper to him and wrote:

Paul: Della will tell you what this is all about, but I want you to have one or more operatives shadow this

10

young woman when she leaves my office. Keep on her trail until I tell you to stop. — Della, try to get an opportunity to look in her purse and see if she really does have a gun.

Mason tore off the sheet from the pad, handed it to Della Street and said, "Take this down to Paul Drake, will you please, Della?"

Della Street, keeping the formal atmosphere which would be compatible with the transmission of a message by paper rather than by word of mouth, said, "Yes, Mr. Mason," and opened the exit door.

Dorrie Ambler crossed good-looking legs. "I suppose you think I'm being very mysterious, Mr. Mason."

"Well, let's put it this way," the lawyer said. "You're a little out of the ordinary."

"I . . . I just have a suspicion that someone is trying to set me up as a — What is it you call a person who is made the victim of a frame-up?"

11

"A fall guy," Mason said, "or a Patsy."

"Since I am not a *guy*," she said, smiling, "I prefer the word Patsy. I don't want to be a Patsy, Mr. Mason."

"I'm sure you don't," Mason told her. "And, by the same token, *I* don't want to be placed in a position which might prove embarrassing to *me*. . . .I take it you gave your name and address to my secretary?"

"Oh, yes, to the receptionist. The young woman at the switchboard."

"That's Gertie," Mason said.

"I gave her the information. I reside at the Parkhurst Apartment, Apartment 907."

"Married, single, divorced?"

"Single."

"Well," Mason said, "you must have people there who can vouch for your identity — the manager of the apartment, for instance."

She nodded.

"How long have you lived there?"

"Oh . . . let me see. . . .Some six months, I guess."

"You have a driving license?" Mason asked.

"Certainly."

"May I see it, please?"

She opened her handbag, holding it in such a way that Mason could not see down into the interior, then took out a purse and from that extracted a driving license.

Mason studied the name, the residence, the description, said, "This was issued five months ago."

"That's right, that was my birthday," she said, and smiled. "You know how old I am now, Mr. Mason.

The lawyer nodded. "This being a California license, there is a thumbprint on it."

"I know."

"So your objection to having your fingerprints taken was at least partially overcome by —"

"Don't misunderstand me, Mr. Mason," she said. "I have no objection to having my fingerprints taken. It's simply that the idea of having them taken and sent to the FBI . . ."

She shuddered.

"We can make a perfect identification from this thumbprint," Mason said.

"Oh," she said, and looked at her thumb. "Are *you* a fingerprint expert, Mr. Mason?"

"No," Mason said, "but Paul Drake is, and I know a little something about comparing prints."

"I see."

"Do you have any other scars?" Mason asked. "Any other operations?"

She smiled. "Just the appendectomy. It's so recent I'm conscious of it all the time."

Drake's code knock sounded on the outer door, and Mason crossed the room to admit Della Street and Paul Drake.

Drake bowed.

She smiled, said "How are you, Mr. Drake."

Mason said, "We have a peculiar situation here, Paul. This young woman wants to have a witness who can establish her identity. She wants you to take a good look at her and she even wants to go so far as to show the scar of a recent operation for the removal of her appendix.''

''I see,'' Drake said gravely.

''And,'' Mason went on, ''I have explained to her that since it now appears she has a California driving license with her thumbprint on it, that's all that will be necessary to compare her thumbprint with the print on the driving license.''

''Well now,'' Drake said, ''a thumbprint is, of course, identification, but on the other hand if she wants to —''

''I do,'' she interposed. ''I don't like fingerprints. That is, I don't like the idea of being fingerprinted. However, if you would like to compare my thumbprint with the print on the license, here's my thumb. But I *don't* want to make fingerprints. I just don't like the idea of getting ink all over my fingers and feeling like a criminal. . . .Can you compare the thumb itself with the print and tell?''

Drake gravely took a small magnifying glass from his pocket, moved over to sit beside her.

"Permit me," he said as she produced the driving license. He gently took her hand in his, held the thumb under the magnifying glass, then looked at the print on the driver's license.

"I have to make a transposition this way," he said, "and it's a little difficult. It would simplify things if you'd . . ."

"No ink," she said, laughing nervously.

"It just means I'll be a little longer," Drake said.

Della Street winked at Perry Mason.

Drake moved his glass back and forth from the thumb to the print on the driver's license, then looked up at Perry Mason and nodded. "All right," he said, "check. You're Dorrie Ambler. But, of course," he added hastily, "we'll check on the appendicitis operation."

She got to her feet abruptly, moved over to a corner of the room.

"I'll get away from the windows," she said.

She slipped off her jacket, raised her blouse to show a small strip of bare skin, then became suddenly self-conscious and pulled it back down.

"Actually," Mason said, "the thumbprint is enough."

"No, no," she said, "I want you to . . ." She broke off, laughing nervously, "After all," she said, "I suppose a lawyer is like a doctor and I think nothing of being examined by my doctor. Well, here goes."

She pulled a zipper at the side of her skirt, slipped her waistband down and pulled her blouse up.

She stood there for a second or two, letting them view smooth, velvety skin, its beauty marred by an angry red line, then suddenly shook her head, pulled the skirt into position and pulled up the zipper.

"Heavens," she said, "I don't know why, but I just feel horribly undressed."

"Well, we've seen it," Drake said, "and in a few months the color will leave that scar and you'll hardly know it's there."

"You can identify me?" she asked.

"Well," Drake said, smiling, "with that thumb and that appendectomy scar I think I can make a pretty good identification if I have to."

"That, she said, "is all I want."

While she had been fumbling with her clothes, Della Street had swiftly opened Dorrie Ambler's handbag, looked inside, snapped the bag shut and then catching Mason's eye, nodded to him.

"All right, Paul," Mason said significantly, "I guess that's all. You're a witness. You can make the identification."

"Perhaps it would help," Drake said, "if I knew what this was all about."

"It would help," Dorrie Ambler said, "if *I* knew what it was all about. All I know is that either I have a double or I'm being groomed as a double for someone else and I'm — I'm afraid."

"How are you being groomed?" Mason asked.

"I've been given these clothes to wear," she said, flouncing the skirt up in such a way that it showed a neat pair of legs well up the thighs. "I've even been given the stockings, the shoes, skirt, jacket, blouse, underwear, everything, and told to wear them, and I'm following certain instructions."

Mason said, "Are there any cleaning marks on those clothes?"

"I haven't looked."

"It might be a good plan to look," Mason said, "but it probably would take fluorescent light."

She said, "I — I'm doing something on my own, Mr. Mason, and I'll be back later on."

"Just what do you contemplate doing?" Mason asked.

She shook her head. "You wouldn't approve," she said, "and therefore you wouldn't let me do it, but I'm going to force the issue out into the open."

Abruptly she picked up her handbag, looked at her watch, turned to Mason and said, "I presume your secretary handles the collections."

Mason said to Della Street, "Make a ten-dollar charge, Della, and give Miss Ambler a receipt."

Della said, "This way, please," and led the client out of the office.

Mason and Drake exchanged glances.

"You've got a man on the job?" Mason asked.

"Jerry Nelson," Drake said. "He's one of the best in the business. It just happened he was in my office making a report on another assignment when Della came in with your note. I also have a second man in a car at the curb. . . . Boy, that's a dish!"

Mason nodded.

"What do you suppose is eating her?" Drake asked.

"I don't know," Mason said. "We'll find out. Probably someone is grooming her for a double in a divorce action. Let me know just as soon as your men have a definite report."

"She'll just go back to her apartment now," Drake said.

Mason shook his head. "I have a peculiar idea, Paul, she's going someplace with a very definite plan of action, and she has a gun in her purse."

"The deuce she does!" Drake exclaimed.

Mason nodded. "Gertie spotted it when she was in the outer office, and Della confirmed it by taking a peek in her purse while you were studying feminine anatomy."

"Well," Drake said, "next time you have a client who wants to do a strip tease, be sure to call on me."

Della Street entered the office.

"She's gone?" Mason asked.

Della Street nodded.

"What about the gun?"

"I didn't have time to do more than just give it a quick look, but there aren't any bullets in it."

"You mean it's empty?" Mason asked.

"No. The shells are in the gun. You can see them by looking down the cylinder, but there aren't any bullets in the shells, just caps of blue paper at the end of the cartridge."

"Blank cartridges!" Mason exclaimed.

"I guess that's what they are," Della

Street said. "It's a small pistol. It looks like a twenty-two caliber."

Drake gave a low whistle.

"She gave you ten dollars and you gave her a receipt?" Mason asked Della Street.

"For services rendered," Della Street said. "Then she *wanted* to give me a hundred dollars as a retainer on future services. I told her I wasn't authorized to accept that, that she'd have to talk with you; so she said never mind, she'd let it go, and hurried out of the office saying she had a time schedule that she had to meet."

"Well," Mason said thoughtfully, "let's hope that schedule doesn't include a murder."

"We're having her shadowed," Paul Drake said. "She won't lose my men. They'll know where she goes and what she does."

"Of course," Mason said thoughtfully, "she can't commit a murder with blank cartridges, but something tells me your report from Jerry Nelson and his assisant is going to be somewhat out of the ordinary. Let me know as soon as you hear from your men, Paul.''

Chapter Two

It was shortly after one-thirty that afternoon when Paul Drake gave his code knock on the door of Mason's private office.

Mason nodded to Della Street. "Let Paul in, Della. He'll have some news."

Della Street opened the door.

Paul Drake said, "Hi, Beautiful," and ushered a chunky, competent-looking man into the office.

"This is Jerry Nelson, one of my operatives," he said. "Jerry, this is Della Street, Mr. Mason's confidential secretary, and Perry Mason. Now I want you to tell these people what happened just as you told it to me."

Drake turned to Mason and said apologetically, "I got this over the telephone. It sounded so cockeyed I told Jerry to dash in and report personally. Now then, I'm turning him over to you all. Go ahead, Jerry.''

Mason smiled and said, ''Sit down, Nelson, and let's have the story.''

Nelson said, ''I know you people are going to think I'm a little screwy but I'm going to tell you exactly what happened.

''Paul Drake told me there was a woman in your office that you wanted shadowed; that I was to pick her up in the elevator; that another operative would be waiting with a car in front of the entrance; that there would be a vacant taxicab waiting just in case anything went wrong. I gathered it was an important job of tailing so I wanted to be on my toes. Drake said we weren't to let her out of our sight no matter what happened.''

Mason nodded.

''Okay,'' Nelson said. ''This young woman left the office. She was above five feet three, somewhere in her early twenties, had chestnut hair, hazel eyes.

She wore a green and brown plaid suit and a green blouse —''

''Now, wait a minute,'' Mason said, ''we know all about her appearance.''

''I know, I know,'' Drake interrupted, ''but get this thing straight, Perry. We want to be sure of our facts.''

''All right, go ahead,'' Mason said.

''Well, anyway,'' Nelson said, ''I got aboard the elevator with this young woman. My partner was waiting out in front.

''She wanted a cab. The cab that we were holding at the curb had its flag down and she tried to get that. The driver pointed to his flag and she started to argue with him but just then another Yellow came along and she flagged it down.

''I was still playing it cautious because we didn't know what was going to happen. The only orders we had were to see that she didn't get out of our sight, and to spare no expense — so I jumped in the cab that we had waiting at the curb, and my buddy pulled out in his car and both of us followed the cab

26

which had been taken by the girl.

"What's more, we had the number on the cab ahead and a twenty-dollar bill got my cabdriver to radio in to the dispatcher and ask him where this cab was going as soon as he got a report.

"The report came in in about two minutes. The cab-driver said he was headed for the airport.

"So both of us tagged along behind and sure enough she went right to the airport without any attempt to shake off any shadows or even paying the slightest attention to what was happening behind her.

"Those cabdrivers get pretty sharp in watching traffic and I felt the cabdriver might be keeping an eye out behind, so I had my cab drop back and the other operative moved in close behind. Then after a while the other operative dropped back and my cab moved up. Between us we kept her in sight all the way."

"All the way where?" Mason asked.

"To the airport."

"Then what?"

"Then she just stuck around."

"How long?"

"Over an hour," the operative said. "She was waiting for something and I guess I was maybe dumb that I didn't pick up what it was, but because I thought she might be trying something shifty I kept my eye on *her* and didn't try to look around too much at the scenery."

"What are you getting at?" Mason said.

"Well, I'd better tell you just the way it happened. You see, when two operatives are working on a case that way, one of them has to be in charge, and because of seniority I was the one to call the shots on this deal. I probably should have had my colleague keeping a look around the place but, as I say, I thought this babe might be trying something shifty so we were keeping our eyes on her."

"What happened?" Mason asked.

"All of a sudden she jumped up, ran over to the newsstand, shouted, 'This isn't a stick-up,' pulled a revolver out of her handbag and fired three shots.

"It was so darned sudden and so completely, utterly senseless that it caught me flat-footed."

"Now, wait a minute," Mason said. "You said that she said, 'This *isn't* a stick-up'?"

"That's right. I was within ten feet of her and I heard her distinctly."

"Go on," Mason said. "What happened? Did you grab her?"

"Not me. I was like everyone else. People stood there just frozen in their tracks. It was one of the darncdcst sights I ever saw, just as though you had been watching a motion picture and all of a sudden the thing stopped and the picture froze on the screen.

"One minute everybody was hurrying around, bustling here and there; people sitting waiting for planes, people buying tickets, people moving back and forth; and then *wham!* Everything stopped and people just stood in their tracks."

"And what about the young woman?"

"The young woman didn't stand in *her* tracks," Neslon said. "She brandished the gun, whirled, and made

29

for the ladies' rest room.

"Now, as far as I'm concerned there's a brand-new crime angle. You have a lot of guards around an airport, and police on duty, but there was no police*woman* immediately available.

"So here's a babe with a gun, barricaded in the women's rest room, and who's going after her?"

"You?" Mason asked, his eyes twinkling.

"Not me," Nelson said. "Facing a crazy woman with a gun is one thing, and facing irate women who have been disturbed in a rest room is another, and when you add the two together you've got too many risks for any mere man. I just stood around where I could watch the door of the rest room."

"And what happened?"

"Well, a couple of cops came running up and held a conference and seemed to be as perplexed about the situation as I was. Then they evidently decided to go through with it and started for the rest room. About that time the door opened and this babe came walking out, just as cool as you please.''

''With a gun?''

''I'm telling you,'' Nelson said, ''she came out just as cool as a cucumber — just like any normal woman who had been powdering her nose and was emerging to take a look at the bulletin board and see just when her plane was scheduled to depart.''

''What happened?'' Mason asked.

''Well, the officers hadn't seen her when she fired the gun so they didn't recognize her when she came out. She walked right past them and it wasn't until one of the bystanders yelled, 'There she is!' that one of the officers turned.

''By that time three or four of the bystanders were pointing their fingers and yelling, 'That's her! Grab her!' and then everybody started to run.''

''Then what happened?''

''You've never seen anything like it,'' Nelson said. ''This woman stood there with the most utterly bewildered expression on her face, looking around to see what it was all about.

"One of the officers came up and grabbed her and for a moment she was startled, then she was indignant and demanded to know what it was all about. Then a crowd gathered and a lot of people started talking all at once."

"What about the gun?" Mason asked.

"The gun had been left in the rest room. A woman came out and handed the officer the gun. It had slid across the floor and scared this women to death. The officers asked our woman if she'd mind if they looked in her handbag and she told them to go ahead. Naturally they couldn't search *her* but they did look in her handbag. Then one of the officers opened the gun and looked at it and seemed more puzzled than ever. He said something to his companion, and the other fellow looked at the gun.

"Now, I don't think anyone there heard what the officers said except me. I was right up at the officer's elbow and I heard him say, 'They're blanks.' "

"How many shots were fired?" Mason asked.

"Three."

"Then what?" Mason asked.

"All of a sudden this women smiled at the officer, said, 'All right, let's get it over with. I just wanted a little excitement. I wanted to see what would happen.' "

"And she admitted firing the shots?"

"She admitted firing the shots," Nelson said. "Well, that was all there was to it. The officers took her into custody. They gave her an opportunity to go to Headquarters in a private police car. We tried to tag along, but you know the way the officers handle things when they are arresting a woman."

"What do you mean?" Mason asked.

"They play it safe," Nelson said. "A woman is always in a position to claim that officers made advances and all that sort of stuff, so whenever they arrest a woman they use their radio telephone to telephone Headquarters, giving the time and location, and stating that they are on their way in with a woman prisoner. Then the dispatcher notes the time and the place and then as soon as the officers get to the place where they're booking the prisoner they check in on time and place.

"The idea is to show that considering the distance traversed, there was absolutely no time for amorous dalliance. So when they have a woman prisoner they're taking in, they really cover the ground.

"They didn't use the red light and siren but they were driving just too damned fast for us to keep up. I got my colleague and we tried our best. We followed the car for . . . oh, I guess three or four miles, and then they pulled through a signal just as it was changing and we lost them."

"So what did you do?" Mason asked.

"So I telephoned to Drake and told him generally what had happened, and Drake told me to come on in and report to him in person."

Mason looked at Drake.

"That's it," Drake said. "That's what happened."

Mason looked at his watch. "Well," he said, "under those circumstances I assume that our client will be asking for

34

an attorney and we'll be hearing from her within the next few minutes.''

Drake said, ''Evidently she had this thing all planned, Perry, and she was just coming to you to get you retained in advance. I thought you should know.''

''I certainly should,'' Mason said.

Drake said to Nelson, ''Well, Jerry, I guess that covers the situation. We've done all the damage we can do.''

''The point is, Mr. Mason,'' Nelson said, ''if anything happens I'm in an embarrassing position.''

''What do you mean?''

''The officers took my name and address. I had to give them one of my cards. My associate saw what was happening and managed to duck out of the way, but I was standing right there and one of the bystanders said to the officer, 'This man was standing right by me and he saw the whole thing,' so the officer turned to me and said, 'What's your name?' and I didn't dare to stall around any because I knew that they'd get me sooner or later and if they found I was a private detective and had been a little reluctant about giving them the information they wanted, they'd have put two and two together and figured right away I was on a case. So I just acted as any ordinary citizen would and gave the officer my name and address."

"Did he check it in any way?"

"Yes. He asked to see my driver's license."

"So he has your name and address."

"Right."

"And if you were called as a witness you'd have to testify to the things that you've told me here."

"That's right."

"Well," Mason said,' "if you're called as a witness you'll have to tell the truth. But I want you to remember that she said that it was *not* a stick-up."

"That's the thing I can't understand," Nelson said. "She walked over toward the newsstand, opened her purse, caught the eye of the girl behind the counter at the newsstand, jerked out the gun, said, 'This *isn't* a stick-up' and then bang! bang! bang! Then she turned and dashed into the women's room."

"But you can swear if you have to that she said it was *not* a stick-up."

"Very definitely. But I guess I'm about the only one that heard it because she said *isn't* and I'll just bet about half of the people — in fact, I guess all of the people — who were around, would swear that she said, 'This *is* a stick-up.' "

"Well, that *isn't* might be rather important," Mason said, "in view of the fact that there were only blank cartridges in the gun. . . . You heard one of the officers say that they were blanks?"

"That's right."

"Okay," Mason said, "I guess that's all there is to it."

Nelson got up and shook hands. "I'm mighty glad to meet you, Mr. Mason. I'm sorry that I may be a witness against you — that is, against your side of the case."

"What do you mean, against?" Mason asked. "You may be one of the best witnesses I have."

Drake, holding the door open for Nelson, said, "You get more goofy cases, Perry, than anyone else in the business.''

"Or more goofy clients," Mason said.

In the doorway Jerry Nelson paused and shook his head. "That's the thing I can't understand," he said. "That woman, when she came out, was the most perfectly poised woman you have ever seen in your life. She acted just completely natural. You wouldn't have thought she even knew what a gun was, let alone having just caused a commotion with one."

"You can't always tell about women," Drake said.

Mason grinned. "You can't *ever* tell about women, Paul."

Chapter Three

An atmosphere of tense expectancy hung over Perry Mason's office until a few minutes before five o'clock when Perry Mason said, "Well, Della, I guess our client has decided she doesn't need an attorney — and I'm hanged if I know why."

"Do you suppose they've been interrogating her and won't let her get to a phone to put through a call?"

"I don't know," Mason said. "I can think of a lot of explanations but none of them is logical. However, I'm not going to worry about it. Let's close up shop, go home and call it a day. We should have closed the office at four-thirty and — Wait a minute, Della, it's almost five. Let's tune in on the five o'clock

39

newscast and see if there is some mention made of what happened. It'll be worth something to find out whether I'm going to have to try to defend a client on a charge of shooting up an airport with blank cartridges.''

''About the only defense to that would be not guilty by reason of insanity,'' Della Street said.

Mason grinned.

Della Street brought out the portable radio, tuned it in to the station and promptly at five o'clock twisted the knob, turning up the volume.

There were comments on the international situation, on the stock market, and then the announcer said, ''The local airport was thrown into a near panic today when an attractive young woman brandished a revolver, shouted 'This is a stick-up!' and then proceeded to fire three shots before retreating into the women's rest room.

''While police were organizing to storm the citadel, the woman in question casually emerged. Upon being identified by spectators and taken into custody by the police, the woman at first professed her innocence, then finally smilingly admitted that she had done the act as a prank. Frankly skeptical, police soon determined two facts which lent strong support to the young woman's statement. One fact was that the revolver was loaded only with blank cartridges and apparently the three shells which had been fired were blanks. The other fact was that an inspection of the woman's driving license identified her as Minerva Minden, who has been designated in the past by at least one newpaper as the madcap heiress of Montrose.

"Miss Minden has from time to time paid visits to Police Headquarters; once for deliberately smashing dishes in a restaurant in order to get the attention of a waiter; once for reckless driving and resisting an officer; once for driving while intoxicated; in addition to which she has received several citations for speeding.

"The young heiress seemed to regard the entire matter as something in the nature of a lark, but Municipal Judge Carl Baldwin took a different view. When the defendant was brought before him to fix bail on charges of disturbing the peace and of discharging firearms in a public place, Judge Baldwin promptly proceeded to fix bail at two thousand dollars upon each count.

"A somewhat chastened Miss Minden said she would plead guilty to the charges, put up cash bail and left the courtroom. She is to appear tomorrow morning at nine-thirty for a hearing on her application for probation and for receiving sentence."

The broadcaster then went on to discuss the weather, the barometric pressure and the temperature of the ocean water.

"Well," Della Street said, as she switched off the radio, "would you say our Miss Ambler is a double of Minerva Minden, the madcap heiress?"

Mason's eyes narrowed. "The crime," he said, "was evidently premeditated, and the driving license and the thumbprint were most certainly those of Dorrie Ambler — so now the scar of the appendectomy *may* assume considerable importance.''

''But how?'' Della Street asked. ''What could be the explanation?''

Mason said, ''I can't think of one, Della, but somehow I'm willing to bet . . .''

The lawyer broke off as timid knuckles sounded against the door from his private office to the corridor.

Mason glanced at his watch. ''Fifteen minutes past five. Don't open *that* door, Della. Go out through the door from the reception room and tell whoever it is that the office is closed for the day, that I'm not available; to telephone tomorrow morning at nine o'clock and ask you for an appointment.''

Della Street nodded, slipped out of Mason's private office into the reception room.

A moment later she was back. ''Guess who?'' she asked.

''Who?'' Mason asked.

''Dorrie Ambler.''

''Did she see you?''

43

Della Street shook her head. "I just opened the door from the reception room into the corridor and started to step out when I saw her. I thought perhaps you'd want to talk with her even if it is after hours."

Mason grinned, stepped to the door and opened it just as the young woman was dejectedly turning away.

"Miss Ambler," Mason said.

She jumped and whirled.

"The office is closed," Mason said, "and I was on the point of leaving for the night, but if it's a matter of some importance I'll see you briefly."

"It's a matter of great importance," she said.

"Come in," Mason invited, holding the door open.

Della Street smiled and nodded.

"Sit down," Mason invited. And then when she had complied, said, "So you're really Minerva Minden, sometimes referred to as the madcap heiress of Montrose."

She met his eyes with a steady frank gaze. "I am *not!*" she said.

Mason shook his head, his manner that of a parent reproving a mendacious child who persists in an incredible falsehood. "I'm afraid your denial isn't going to carry much weight, but this is your party. You wanted to see me upon a matter of some importance and it's only fair to remind you that you're paying for my time. Moreover, one of the factors in fixing my charges is the financial ability of the client to pay. Now, you just go ahead and take all the time you want. Tell me any fairy story you want me to hear and remember that it's costing you money, lots of money."

"You don't understand," she said.

"I'm afraid I do," Mason told her. "Now I'm going to tell you something else. When you were here in the office I knew that you had a gun in your purse. I hired a detective to shadow you. You were shadowed up to the airport, and a detective was standing within a few feet of you when you staged that demonstration.

"Now then, Miss Minden, I'd like to know just what your game is, what you have in mind and how you expect me to fit into the picture.

"For your further information, I don't like to have clients lie to me, and I feel that after I have heard your story there is every possibility that I will not care to have you continue as a client."

She was watching him with wide eyes. "You've had me shadowed?"

Mason nodded.

"You knew there was a gun in my purse?"

Again the lawyer nodded.

She said, "Thank God!"

Mason's face showed his surprise.

"Look," she said, "I'm *not* Minerva Minden. I'm Dorrie Ambler, and the thing I did this afternoon at the airport was for the purpose of forcing Minerva Minden to tell what was really going on, but she was too smart for me. She outwitted me."

Mason's eyes showed dawning interest. "Go ahead," he said.

She said, "It all started four days ago when I answered an ad for a young woman, either trained or untrained, who

46

could do special work. The ad specified that applicants must be between twenty-two and twenty-six years of age, that they must be exactly five feet three inches tall, weighing not less than a hundred and ten pounds nor more than a hundred and fifteen pounds, and offered a salary of a thousand dollars a month.''

Della Street flashed a glance at Perry Mason. ''I saw that ad,'' she said. ''It only ran for one day.''

''Go ahead,'' Mason said to Dorrie Ambler.

''Someone mailed me a copy of the ad and I applied for that job,'' she said, ''and so did scads of other people — and there was something phony about it.''

''Keep talking,'' Mason said, his eyes now showing keen interest.

''Well, to begin with, we were asked to go to a suite in a hotel in order to make application. A very efficient young woman sat a desk in a room in that suite, on which had been pasted a sign, PERSONNEL MANAGER.

''Opening out of this suite were two

rooms. One of them had a label, RED ROOM. The other had a label, BLACK ROOM. The young woman at the desk would give each applicant a ticket. The red tickets went to the red room, the black tickets went to the black room.''

''Then what?'' Mason asked.

''As far as the red room is concerned I don't know for sure, but I did talk with one girl who was given a ticket to the red room. She went in there and sat down and she said there were about twenty young women who came in and sat down in that room. They waited for about fifteen minutes and then a woman came to them and told them that there was no need for them to wait any longer; the situation was no longer open.''

''All right,'' Mason said, ''you were given a ticket to the black room. What happened there?''

''Apparently only about one applicant out of fifteen or twenty got a black ticket. I was one of them. I went in there and sat down and one other girl came in while I was there.

''After I'd been there for ten or fifteen

minutes, a door opened and a man said, 'Step this way, please.'

"I went into still another room in the suite — heavens, that suite in the hotel must have cost a small fortune."

"Who was the man?" Mason asked.

"He said he was a vice president in charge of personnel, but the way he acted *I* think he was a lawyer."

"What makes you think so?"

"The way he threw questions at me."

"What sort of questions?"

"He had me sit down and asked me a lot about my background, all about my parents, where I'd been employed, and so forth. Then he asked me to stand up and walk around. He was watching me like a hawk."

"Passes?" Mason asked.

"I don't think that was what he had in mind," she said, "but he certainly was looking me over."

"And then?"

"Then he asked me how my memory was and if I could give quick answers to questions and a lot of things like that, and then said, 'What were you doing on the evening of the sixth of September?'

"Well, that hadn't been *too* long ago, and after thinking a minute I told him that I had been in my apartment. I hadn't had a date that night although it had been a Saturday, and he asked me who was with me and I told him no one. He wanted to know if I'd been there the entire evening and I told him I had. Then he asked me if I'd had any visitors at all during the evening, or had had any phone calls, and a lot of personal questions of that sort, and then asked me for my telephone number and told me that I was being seriously considered for the job."

"Did he tell you what kind of a job it was?"

"He said it was going to be a rather peculiar job, that I was going to have to undergo intensive training in order to hold down the position but that I would be paid during the period of training. He said that the pay was at the rate of a thousand dollars a month, that the position would be highly confidential, and that I would be photographed from time to time in various types of clothing.''

''Did he say what type?'' Mason asked.

''No, he didn't. Of course I became suspicious right away and told him there was no use wasting each other's time, did he mean I'd be posing in the nude, and he said definitely not, that it was perfectly legitimate and aboveboard, but that I'd be photographed from time to time in various types of clothing; that the people I was to work for didn't want posed photographs. They wanted pictures of young women on the street, that I wasn't to be alarmed if someone pointed a camera at me and took pictures of me on the street, that that would be done often enough so that I would lose all self-consciousness.''

''And then what?''

''Well, then I went home and after I'd been there about two hours the telephone rang and he told me I'd been selected for the position.''

''You were unemployed at the time?'' Mason asked.

"As it happened, I was. I'd been foolish enough to think I could support myself by selling encyclopedias on a door-to-door basis."

"Couldn't you?" Mason asked.

"I suppose I could," she said, "if I'd absolutely *had* to. But I just didn't have the stamina for it."

"What do you mean?"

"You ring doorbells," she said. "Someone comes to the door. You only get invited in about once out of five times if you're *really* good. If you're not, you're apt not to get invited in at all."

"If you do, what happens?"

"Then you get in and make your sales pitch and answer questions and arrange for a follow-up."

"A follow-up?" Mason asked.

"Yes, you call during the daytime and the woman doesn't like to take on that much of an obligation without consulting her husband. So if you've really made a good pitch you're invited to come back in the evening when he's home."

"And you didn't like it?" Mason

asked.

"I liked it all right but it was just too darned exhausting. In order to stay with a job of that sort you have to develop a shell. You become as thoroughly professional as a — as a professional politician."

"So you quit?" Mason asked.

"Well, I didn't exactly quit but I made up my mind that I'd only work mornings. Afternoons are rather nonproductive anyway because so many times you find women who are planning on going to a club meeting or have got their housework caught up and want to do something else during the afternoon. They are either not going to give you the time to let you talk with them or they're impatient when they do talk with you."

"I see," Mason said. "Go ahead."

"All right," she said. "I went back to my apartment. It was a day when I was resting. I didn't feel too full of pep anyway and I was taking life easy when the phone rang and I was told that I'd been selected and asked to come back to the hotel."

"Then what?"

"Then I went to the hotel and everything had changed. There was no longer the woman at the desk, but this man was sitting in the parlor of the suite and he told me to sit down and he'd tell me something about the duties of the job.

"He gave me the plaid suit I was wearing this morning, the blouse, the stockings, even the underthings. He told me that this was to be my first assignment, that he wanted me to put on these clothes and wear them until I got accustomed to them, that I was to get them so they looked as though they were a part of my personality, and I was not to be at all self-conscious. He suggested that I could step in to the bedroom and try the clothes on.

"Did you?" Mason asked.

"I did after some hesitancy," she said, "and believe me, I saw that both doors into that bedroom were locked. I just had a feeling that I had got into something that was a little too much for me."

54

"All right," Mason said, "go on. What happened? Did he make passes?"

"No, I had the deal sized up a hundred per cent wrong. The man was a perfect gentleman. I put on the clothes and came out. He looked me over, nodded approvingly and then gave me a hat and told me I was to wear that hat. He told me that my duties would be very light for the first few days, that I was to sleep late the next morning, that I was to get up and have had breakfast by ten-thirty; that I was to go to the intersection of Hollywood and Vine and cross the street fifty times. At the end of that time I was free to go home."

"Crossing the street from what direction?" Mason asked.

"He said it didn't make any difference. Just walk back and forth across the street, being careful to obey the signals, and that I was to remember not to pay any attention to anybody who might be there with a camera."

"Was somebody there?" Mason asked.

"Yes, a man was there with a camera.

55

He took pictures mostly of me but occasionally he would take a picture of someone else.''

''And you walked back and forth?'' Mason asked.

''That's right.

''The clothes fit you?''

''As though they'd been made for me. They were the ones I wore this morning.''

''Now then,'' Mason said. ''This is an important point. Were these clothes new or had they been worn?''

''They were new. They hadn't been sent to the cleaner as nearly as I could tell. They had, however, evidently been made specially. There were even some bits of the basting threads left in the seams.''

''Did you,'' Mason asked, ''ever see any of the pictures?''

''No, just the man with the camera.''

''All right, go on. What happened?''

''I was told to telephone a certain unlisted number for instructions. I telephoned the number and was told that everything was okay. I had done all that

I needed to do for the day and I could have the rest of the time off.''

"Then what?" Mason asked.

She said, "I did a little detective work on my own."

"Such as what?"

"I called the unlisted number, disguised my voice and asked for Mac. The man said I had the wrong number and asked what number I was calling and I gave him the number. It was, of course, the correct number. He said I had made a mistake and had the wrong number. I told him that I didn't, that I knew the number Mac had given me. So then he started getting a little mysterious and I think a little concerned. He said, 'Look, this is a detective agency, Billings and Compton. We don't have any Mac working for us,' and I said, 'A dectective agency, huh?' And slammed up the phone."

"So then what?"

"Then," she said, "I looked up the address of Billings and Compton Detective Agency and decided to go up there and ask for a showdown. I didn't know just what I was getting into.''

''And what happened?'' Mason asked.

''I never went in,'' she said. ''I — Well, something happened and I thought I saw the picture.''

''What was it that happened?''

''I drove my car up there. There's a parking lot right next door to the building. I put my car in the parking lot and was just getting out when I saw my double.''

''Your what?''

''My double.''

''Now,'' Mason said, ''I'm beginning to get the picture. Just what did your double look like?''

''She looked *exactly* like me. She was dressed exactly the same way, and there was more than a superficial resemblance. It was really startling. She was my height, my build, my complexion, and of course since we were wearing identical clothes — well, I had to stop and do a double take. I thought I was looking at myself in the mirror.''

''And what was your double doing?''

''Standing in line, waiting for her car

to be brought to her."

"And what did you do?"

"I kept on doing detective work. I stopped my car and continued to sit in it and when the man gave me a parking ticket I just kept on sitting there until I saw her car being delivered and I got the license number of her car, WBL 873."

"So then you looked up the registration?" Mason asked.

"That's right."

"And the registration was Minerva Minden?"

"Right."

"And then?" Mason asked.

"Well, then I reported for work the next day and I was told to go to another locality. This time it was Sunset and La Brea and I was to cross the street fifty times."

"You did that?"

"Yes."

"And the photographer was there?"

"Part of the time the photographer was there, part of the time he drove by in an automobile. Once I'm certain that he had a motion-picture camera in the

59

automobile when he stopped and parked the car and took motion pictures of me.''

''And then what?''

''Then I called the unlisted number again and was told that my work was done for the day, that I could relax, have cocktails and dinner and that there would be no more calls on my time.''

''So what did you do?''

She said, ''I came to the conclusion that I was being groomed for something and that I was going to be what you called a Patsy.''

''Perhaps Minerva Minden wants an alibi for something,'' Mason said.

''I've thought of all that,'' she said. ''We're not twins but there certainly is a startling resemblance. But wait until you hear what happened the next day.''

''Okay, what did happen?''

''So,'' she said, ''the next day I was told to go to Hollywood Boulevard and Western, that I was to cross the street, walk one block along Hollywood Boulevard, wait ten minutes, walk back, cross Western, then cross Hollywood

Boulevard and go up the other side of the street; wait ten minutes, then come back down and retrace my steps. I was to keep that up at ten-minute intervals for two hours."

"You did it?" Mason asked.

"I only did part of it."

"What part?"

"About the third time — I think it *was* the third time I was making the trip up Hollywood Boulevard I passed a store and a little girl cried out, 'Momma, there she is now!' "

"Then what happened?"

"A woman ran to the door and took a look at me and then suddenly dashed out of the store and started following me."

"What did you do?"

"I walked up Hollywood Boulevard just as I had been instructed, and the photographer was there at the corner and took a picture of me, and I think of the woman following me. Then suddenly I got frightened. I jumped in my car which I'd left parked on the side street and drove away as fast as I could."

"That was when?"

"That was yesterday."

"And then what?"

"Then I made it a point to look up Minerva Minden, and the more I saw of the thing the more I was satisfied that I was being groomed as a double for some sinister purpose. So I made up my mind that I'd just bring matters to a head."

"By shooting up the airport?"

"I decided I'd do something so darned spectacular that the whole business would be brought out into the open."

"So what did you do?"

"I rang up the number for instructions. They told me I didn't need to do anything today. I learned that Miss Minden was taking a plane for New York. I checked her reservation. So I got all prepared and went to the airport.

"She was wearing the same clothes that I was and — well, I got the pistol, loaded it with blank cartridges, had you inspect my appendicitis operation scar so there could be no question — Oh, it's terribly mixed up, Mr. Mason, but it was the best way I could think of, of —"

"Never mind all that," Mason said. "Tell me what happened."

"Well, I went down to the airport. I waited until Minerva showed up and went into the women's room, then I jumped up, grabbed the gun, yelled. 'This *isn't* a stick-up' and shot into the air. Then I dashed into the women's room. There are several stalls in there for showers where a person can put in a coin, get a shower, towels and all of that. Those stalls insure complete privacy. So I ran into the rest room, skidded the gun along the floor, put the coin in the slot and went into the shower.

"I felt sure that Minerva would walk into the trap, and of course she did."

"You mean she came out of the rest room and was identified?"

"She came out of the rest room and was promptly identified. People came crowding around her and the cops started questioning her and of course that gave her a pretty good background of what had happened."

"And at that time you thought she'd

say that she hadn't done it at all, that it was someone else and the officers would look in the rest room and find you.''

"Well, I wasn't certain that it would go *that* far. I thought that I would have an opportunity to get out of the rest room in the excitement before the officers came in and searched, but what I was totally unprepared for was to have her realize what had happened and with diabolical coolness say that *she* had been the one who had fired the shots.''

Mason looked at his client steadily.

"She *was* the one who fired the shots, wasn't she, Dorrie? And you're working some part of a carefully rehearsed scheme?''

"On my honor, Mr. Mason, I was the one who fired those shots. Minerva was the one who tried to take the blame — and I can tell you how you can prove it in case you absolutely have to. I was afraid that if I said 'This is a stick-up,' that even if the gun had blank cartridges in it I might be guilty of some sort of a felony, of trying to get money by brandishing a firearm or something, so I played it safe by shouting at the top of my voice, 'This *isn't* a stick-up.'

''Now, I know that most of the witnesses heard what they thought they should have heard, and claim the person brandishing the gun said this *is* a stick-up. But if you should ever have to cross-examine them and should ask them if it wasn't a fact that the woman said this *isn't* a stick-up, I'll bet you they would admit that that's what they really heard — but you know how it is. No one wants to come forward and be the first to say the woman said this *isn't* a stick-up. It would make them sound sort of foolish and — well, that's the way it is. No one would want to be the first, but once someone tells the real truth the others will fall in line.''

''Just what did you have in mind?'' Mason asked. ''What do you want *me* to do now?''

She said, ''I want you to protect my interests. I would like to find out what it is that happened on the sixth of September that would have caused someone to go to all this trouble.''

65

"You feel that you were built up as a fall guy, a substitute, a Patsy."

She said, "I'm quite satisfied that I have been built up as a double and am going to be called on to take the blame for something I didn't do. And if you had detectives follow me to the airport, you *know* I was the one who fired those shots and then the woman who came out — this Minerva Minden, did some quick thinking and decided to take the blame rather than let it be known I was her double."

"Would you mind letting me see your driving license again?" Mason asked.

"Certainly not."

She opened her purse, took out her driving license and handed it to Mason.

Mason checked the license, then said, "Let me have your thumb. I'm going to make a comparison."

"Good heavens, but you're suspicious!"

"I'm a lawyer," Mason said. "I hate to have anything slipped over on me."

She immediately extended her thumb.

Mason said, "I know your aversion to

fingerprints so I'll try making a check from the thumb itself.''

He took a magnifying glass from his desk, studied the thumb and the print on the driving license.

''Satisfied?'' she asked.

Mason nodded.

''Now I'll show you the scar.''

''That won't be necessary,'' Mason said. ''I'm convinced.''

''Very well,'' she said. ''Now will you try and find out what it is I'm being framed for? In other words, what sort of a racket I'm mixed up in?''

Mason nodded.

''Now look,'' she told him, ''This is going to take some money. I don't have very much but —''

''Suppose we skip that for the moment,'' Mason said. ''I'll give the case a once-over and then get in touch with you.''

''I'm so . . . so frightened,'' she said.

''I don't think you need to be,'' Mason told her.

''But I'm fighting someone who has

unlimited money, someone who is ruthless and unbelievably clever, Mr. Mason. I'm afraid that even with your help I — Well, I'm afraid they may pin something on me.''

Mason said, ''Call that unlisted number right now and ask the person who answers what your duties are for tomorrow.''

Mason caught Della Street's eye. ''You can call him from this phone,'' he said, ''and I want to listen in and see what the man says.''

She hesitated a moment.

''Any objections?'' Mason asked.

''I'm not supposed to call until later on.''

''Well, let's try it now,'' Mason said. ''Let's see if there's an answer. Miss Street will fix the telephone connection so you're connected with an outside line and you can go right ahead and dial the number.''

Della Street smiled, picked up the telephone, pressed the button and a moment later when a light flashed on the phone, handed the instrument to

Dorrie Ambler.

"Go right ahead," Mason said. "Dial the number."

Dorrie seated herself at Della Street's desk and dialed the number. When she had finished dialing, Mason picked up the telephone to listen.

A man's voice said, "Yes? Hello."

"Who is this?" Dorrie Ambler asked.

"Who are you calling?"

Dorrie Ambler gave the number.

"All right, what do you want?"

"This is Miss Ambler — Dorrie. I wanted to know what instructions there were for tomorrow."

"Tomorrow," the man's voice said, "you simply sit tight. Do nothing. Take it easy. Go to a beauty shop. Have a good time."

"I do nothing?"

"Nothing."

"And my salary?"

"Goes on just the same," the man said, and hung up.

Dorrie Ambler looked over at Mason as though for instructions and slowly dropped the telephone receiver into its cradle.

"All right," Mason said cheerfully, looking at his watch, "we've got to close up the office and go home, Miss Ambler, and I guess the best thing for you to do is the same."

"Suppose something should happen — there should be some developments. Where can I reach you?"

"I don't have a night number where you can reach me," Mason said, "but if you want to call the Drake Detective Agency which is on this floor and leave a message for me, they'll see that I get it within an hour or so at the latest. . . .You feel something may be going to happen?"

"I don't know. I just have that feeling of dread, of apprehension, of something hanging over my head. Minerva Minden knows what happened, of course, and she's apt to do almost anything. You see, she'll know I've found out she's the one I'm doubling for."

Mason said, "We'll try to find out what it's all about, and don't worry."

"I feel better now that the situation is

in your hands — but I do have a definite feeling that I'm being jockeyed into position for a very devastating experience.''

''Well, we can't do very much until we know more of the facts,'' Mason said.

''And remember, Mr. Mason, I want to pay you. I can get some money. I can raise some. Would five hundred dollars be enough?''

''When can you raise five hundred dollars?'' Mason asked.

''I think I could have it by tomorrow afternoon.''

''You're going to borrow it?''

''Yes.''

''Who from?''

''A friend.''

''A boy friend?''

She hesitated a moment, then slowly nodded.

''And does he know anything about all of this?'' Mason asked.

''No. He knows that I have a rather peculiar job. He's been asking questions but I've been sort of — well, giving

71

indefinite answers. I think any young woman who has training in the business world should learn to keep her mouth tightly closed about the things she observes on the job. I think she should keep them entirely removed from her social life.''

''That's very commendable,'' Mason said. ''You go on home and I'll try and find out something more about all this and then get in touch with you.''

''Thank you *so* much,'' Dorrie Ambler said, and then acting on a sudden impulse, gave him her hand. ''Thank you again, Mr. Mason. You've taken a tremendous load off my shoulders. Good night. Good night, Miss Street.''

She slipped out of the door into the corridor.

''Well?'' Della Street asked.

''Now,'' Mason said, ''we find out what happened at Western and Hollywood Boulevard on September Sixth. Unless I'm very much mistaken, Minerva Minden was driving while intoxicated and became involved in a hit-and-run, and now she wants to confuse the witnesses so they'll make a wrong identification.

"Telephone the traffic department at Headquarters, Della, and see what they have on file for hit-and-run on the sixth."

Della Street busied heself on the phone, made shorthand notes, thanked the person at the other end of the line, hung up and turned to Perry Mason.

"On the night of the sixth," she said, "a pedestrian, Horace Emmett, was struck in the crosswalk at Hollywood Boulevard and Western Avenue. He is suffering from a broken hip. The car which struck him was driven by a young woman. It was a light-colored Cadillac. The woman stopped, sized up the situation, got out of the car, then changed her mind, jumped into the car and drove away. She apparently was intoxicated."

Mason grinned. "Okay, Della. We close up the place and I'll buy you a dinner. Tomorrow we'll see about Minerva Minden. By tomorrow night we'll have a very nice cash settlement for our client, Dorrie Ambler, and a very, very handsome cash settlement for Horace Emmett.

"And we'll let Paul have his man, Jerry Nelson, cover Minerva Minden's hearing tomorrow and see what the judge does to her — and better tell Paul to get all the the dope on that Horace Emmett accident.

Chapter Four

At ten o'clock the next morning Paul Drake's code knock sounded on the door of Mason's private office.

Mason nodded to Della Street, who opened the door for the detective.

"Hi, Beautiful," Paul said. "It does you good to get out and dance. Your eyes look like the depths of a deep pool in the moonlight."

Della Street smiled, said, "And it does you good to sit in an office and drink cold coffee and eat soggy hamburgers. Your mind is filled with matters of romance."

Drake made a wry face. "I can taste that cold coffee yet."

He turned to Perry Mason. "I sent Jerry Nelson down to the hearing on the

75

report for probation and the fixing of sentence in Minerva Minden's case, Perry. I gave him your number and told him to report to me here. I felt that you'd want to know just as soon as I heard from him.''

Mason nodded.

''I held him up a little while,'' Drake said, ''because it wasn't certain that Minerva Minden was going to be in court personally. She might have appeared through an attorney.''

''She's there?'' Mason asked.

''In person, with all her charm,'' Drake said. ''She is adept at showing just enough leg to win the judge over to her side and stop just short of indecent exposure. That's quite a gal.''

Drake looked at his watch. ''We should be hearing from Nelson any minute now.''

''Wasn't there some litigation over the Minden inheritance?'' Della asked.

Drake grinned. ''There was some and there could have been a hell of a lot more. Old Harper Minden left a whale of a fortune and not a single heir in the world that anybody could find until finally some enterprising investigator dug up Minerva.

"Minerva at the time was slinging hash and was something of a problem. She was supposed to be wild in those days. Now that she's got a whole flock of money, she's a quote madcap unquote."

"But Harper Minden wasn't her grandfather, was he?" Mason asked.

"Hell, no. He was related to her through some sort of a collateral relationship, and actually the bulk of the estate is still tied up. Minerva has received a partial distribution of five or six million, but —"

"Before taxes?" Mason asked.

"Proviso in the will that the estate was to pay all taxes," Drake said, "and boy, it was quite a bite. But old Harper sure had it piled up. He had so much money he didn't know how much he had. He had gold mines, oil wells, real estate, the works."

The telephone rang.

"That's probably Jerry now,"

Drake said.

Della answered the phone, nodded to Paul and held out the receiver.

Drake said, "You have an attachment you can put this on a loud-speaker, haven't you, Della?"

She nodded, pressed a button, and put a conference microphone in the middle of Mason's desk.

"All the voices will come in," she said.

Drake, sitting some ten feet from the microphone, said, "Hello, Jerry. Can you hear me?"

"Sure I can hear you," Nelson said, his voice, amplified through a loud-speaker, filling Mason's office.

"You seen this gal yet?" Drake asked.

"Have I seen her?" Jerry said "I'm still gasping for breath."

"That much of a knockout?"

"Not only that much of a knockout, but that much of a resemblance."

"She's really a dead ringer?"

"Well, not exactly a dead ringer but it would easily be possible to get them mixed. Now look, Paul, is there any chance those girls are related? I mean closely related. Does anybody know whether Minerva Minden had a sister?"

"She wasn't supposed to have," Drake said.

"Well, as I remember it," Nelson said, "the thing was mixed up in some kind of litigation. Minerva Minden was able to prove her relationship so she got several million dollars, but the family tree has never been completely uncovered. There was some talk about Minerva's mother having a sister who might have had a child before she died."

"You feel pretty certain the two women are related?" Drake asked.

"I'd bet my last cent they're relatives," Nelson said. "I've never seen anything so completely confusing in my life. The two women look alike, they're built the same way, they have the same mannerisms. Their voices are different and the hair and general coloring is a little different but there's one hell of a resemblance. I don't know what you fellows are working on. I suppose it ties in with that inheritance. There's still twenty or thirty million dollars to be distributed. All I want to say is that you've struck pay dirt.''

''Okay,'' Drake said, glancing at Mason, ''keep that angle under your hat. Where are you now?''

''Up at court.''

''And what's happening?''

''Oh, the usual thing. The judge is looking over his glasses at Minerva and giving her a lecture. He's imposed a five-hundred-dollar fine on each of the two charges, making a total of a thousand dollars, and he's busy now explaining to her that it was touch and go with him whether to give her a jail sentence as well; that he finally decided against it because he feels that in her case it wouldn't do any good. He's read the report of the probation officer, he's heard the application for probation, and despite the vehement requests of the defense attorney, he is going to deny probation and let the fines stand. He feels that it would be unfair to give this

80

defendant probation.''

''Okay,'' Drake said, ''keep on the job and study her as much as possible.''

''Boy, I've studied her!'' Nelson said.

''Okay,'' Drake told him, ''come on up then. Has she noticed you staring?''

''Hell, it's a crowded courtroom,'' Nelson said. ''Everybody's staring.''

''Well, come on up,'' Drake said.

''Okay. 'Bye now.''

''Good-by.''

Della Street pressed the button that turned off the telephone. ''What do you know,'' Drake said, looking at Mason.

''Apparently not half enough,'' Mason said thoughtfully.

''What's the story behind all this, Perry?'' Paul asked.

''Apparently,'' Mason said, ''Minerva Minden wanted a ringer to take a rap for her.''

''The hit-and-run?'' Drake asked.

Mason nodded thoughtfully.

''So what happened?''

''So,'' Mason said, ''you may have noticed an ad in the paper a while ago offering a salary of a thousand dollars a month to a woman who had certain physical qualifications as to age, height, complexion and weight, and could qualify for the job.''

''I didn't notice it,'' Drake said.

''Apparently a lot of people did,'' Mason told him, ''and the women were given an intensive screening. They wanted someone who could wear Minerva Minden's clothes, or clothes that would duplicate hers, and spend some time walking back and forth past the scene of the accident where at least one of the witnesses lived and where an identification would be made.''

''Of the wrong woman?''

''Of the wrong woman,'' Mason said. ''That would let Minerva off the hook. If they subsequently found out it was the wrong woman, the witnesses would have all made at least one demonstrable mistaken identification. That would weaken the prosecution's case tremendously.

''If, on the other hand, the charge stood up against the ringer, then Minerva was in the clear.''

"And they got that good a ringer?" Drake asked incredulously.

Mason nodded. "One of those coincidences, Paul. Apparently some detective agency was looking for a girl of just the right size, build and complexion who could wear Minerva's clothes and could walk back and forth in front of at least one of the witnesses until there was an identification. Then presumably the other witnesses would be called in and they'd all identify the wrong person."

Drake grinned. "Now, wouldn't it be poetic justice, Perry, if this babe put an ad in the paper in order to get herself out of a jam and in so doing had to split up an inheritance of fifty-odd million dollars — and where does that leave us?"

"Sitting right out on the end of some kind of a golden limb," Mason said. "We —"

The telephone rang.

Della Street picked up the instrument, said, "Hello," cupped her hand over the mouthpiece and said to Perry Mason,

"Dorrie Ambler."

Mason made a motion. "Put her on loud-speaker, Della."

A moment later Della Street nodded, and Mason said, "Hello, Miss Ambler."

"Oh, Mr. Mason!" she said, her voice excited. "I know I have no business asking this but *could* you come to my apartment?"

"Why don't you come here?" Mason asked.

"I can't."

"Why not?"

"I'm being watched. I'm being pinned down here."

"Where's here?"

"At the Parkhurst Apartments. Apartment 907."

"What's pinning you down there?"

"There are men — a man out in the corridor, ducking in and out of the broom closet. . . . From the window of my apartment I can see my car where I parked it, and there's another man keeping watch on that car."

"All right," Mason said, "that means the police have got you located and you're going to be picked up on a hit-and-run charge.''

'' A hit-and-run charge?'' she asked.

''That's right. That's what happened on the sixth of September.''

''And you mean that was the thing they've been getting ready to frame me for?'' she asked indignantly. ''I'm supposed to be offered as a sacrifice for that terribly rich woman who —''

''Take it easy, take it easy,'' Mason said. ''This is a telephone and we don't know who may be listening.

''Now look, Miss Ambler, a matter has come up of very, very great importance. I have to see you and I would like to see you right away.''

''But I can't leave. I'm not going to. I'm just absolutely frightened to death.''

''Those people are police officers,'' Mason said. ''They aren't going to hurt you, but they're going to stick around until they're absolutely sure that you're up and dressed and then they're going to come barging in to your apartment and ask you questions about the driving of the automobile and the accident on the sixth of September.''

''Well, what do I tell them?''

''Tell them nothing at the moment,''Mason said. ''We haven't got all our proof together but we're getting it. Tell them you were home on the sixth of September and don't tell them anything else.

''In the meantime we've got to get on the job. Now, where's your car?''

''Downstairs.''

''You said you could see it?''

''Yes.''

''Where is it?''

''At the curb.''

''Isn't there a garage connected with that building?''

''Yes, there are private garages but something happened to the lock on my garage door and my key won't work. However, I don't use the garage much anyway. It hasn't been too well ventilated and there's a mildew smell in there that I don't want to get in my car. Lots of the tenants leave their cars out.''

''All right,'' Mason said. ''I have

something to discuss with you, Miss Ambler. . . . Tell me something, is your father living?"

"No."

"Your mother living?"

"No."

"But you know all about your family?"

"Why are you asking this, Mr. Mason?"

"It's something that has just come up and it may be important."

"Actually, Mr. Mason, I don't know a thing about my family. I was — Well, I was put out for adoption. I think I'm —All right, I may as well tell you, you're my attorney. I'm an illegitimate child."

Mason and Paul Drake exchanged glances.

"How do you know you are?" Mason asked.

"Because I was put out for adoption by my mother and — Well, I've never looked into it. I guess it was just one of those things. I've wondered sometimes who my people really were."

"You've never taken any steps to find out?" Mason asked.

"No. What steps *could* I take?"

"You stay right where you are," Mason said. "I'm coming up. I want to talk to you. I'll have Mr. Drake with me — the detective, you know."

"Oh. . . . Could you come right away, Mr. Mason?"

"I'm coming right now," Mason said.

"I'll be waiting."

"Wait right there," Mason said. "No matter what happens, don't leave."

Mason nodded to Della Street, who punched the button which shut off the phone.

"Come on, Paul," Mason said. He turned to Della Street. "Just as soon as Jerry Nelson comes in, tell him to follow us out there. You have the address. I want Jerry to take another look at this girl and compare her with the other one. It may be we've stumbled onto a red-hot lead."

"A red-hot lead in a fifty-million-dollar jackpot," Drake said. "Boy, wouldn't *that* be a juicy jackpot to hit."

Chapter Five

Drake parked his car in front of the Parkhurst Apartments. Paul Drake and the lawyer cautiously emerged.

"See anyone watching the building or spotting a car, Paul?" Mason asked.

"Not yet," Drake said, his trained eyes moving swiftly from side to side. "Do you know what kind of a car she drives, Perry?"

"No, I don't," Mason said. "She's been a working girl. Probably it'll be a medium-priced model four or five years old."

"Lot of those here," Drake said. "Probably second cars that the wife uses in going shopping while the head of the house takes the good car to work."

"Rather charitable for a bachelor this

morning, aren't you?'' Mason asked.

''Romantic as hell,'' Drake said, his eyes still restlessly searching. ''It must have been something in that bicarbonate of soda I had last night. It *couldn't* have been anything in the hamburger . . . Okay, Perry, the place is clean down here. Not even anyone in a parked car.''

''Okay, let's go up,'' Mason said.

''Better lay our plans, Drake said. ''Suppose this guy in the corridor tries to duck out of sight when we go up there.''

''We go pull him out of hiding and see what makes him tick,'' Mason said.

''If he's a police officer you'll have trouble.''

''If he isn't, he'll have trouble,'' Mason said grimly. ''In any event he'll have some explanations to make. Come on, Paul, let's go.''

They went up in the elevator, got out at the ninth floor and Mason said to Paul, ''You take the left, I'll take the right, Paul. Cover the entire corridor.''

The two men walked down the corridor to the end, then turned, retraced their steps and met again in front of the elevator.

"Anything at your end?" Drake asked.

Mason shook his head.

"Mine's clear."

"All right, let's go talk with her . . . Now remember, Paul, any of this business about the estate is entirely extracurricular. At this time, we aren't going to bring that up. We'll look the situation over. So far I'm retained only for one specific purpose."

"And what is that?" Drake asked.

Mason grinned. "Just to keep her from being a fall guy for something she didn't do. Okay, Paul, here we go."

They advanced to the door of 907.

Mason pressed his finger against the mother-of-pearl button, and chimes sounded on the inside of the apartment.

There was complete silence from the interior.

Mason said. "She certainly should be here." He pressed the button again, listened to the chimes, then knocked on the door.

Drake said, "I can hear something inside, Perry, a dragging sound."

Mason pressed his ear to the door.

"Sounds like something being moved across the floor," he said, and banged peremptorily on the door.

From inside the apartment something fell with a thud that jarred the floor, then a woman screamed and the scream was interrupted as though someone had pressed a hand across her lips.

Mason flung himself against the door. The latch clicked, and the door opened a scant three inches to the end of a brass chain safety lock.

From the interior of the apartment a door banged shut.

"Let's go," Mason said, and slammed his shoulder against the door.

Wood creaked in protest, the chain snapped taut but the door still held.

"Come on," Mason shouted at Drake, "all together — both of us now. Let's *GO!*"

The two men hit the door simultaneously. The screws pulled from the safety lock, and the door slammed wide open, banged against a doorstop, then shivered on its hinges.

Mason and Drake stood for a split second in the doorway looking at the scene of confusion which met their eyes.

The apartment consisted of a living room, a bedroom, bath and kitchen. The door to the bedroom stood open so that it was possible to see the drawers which had been pulled from the bureau, the chest of drawers, and the contents dumped helter-skelter over the floor.

In the living room a man lay sprawled on his back, motionless, in a grotesque sprawl, his mouth sagged open.

Sounds came from behind the closed door which evidently led to the kitchen.

Mason pushed past Paul Drake, ran to hurl himself against the kitchen door.

The door gave an inch or two, then closed itself as Mason backed away for another lunge at the door.

"Come on, Paul," the lawyer shouted, "get this door open!"

Both men flung their weight against the door. Again the door opened an inch or two and again closed.

"Somebody's braced against the door on the other side," Drake said. "Watch out! They may start shooting through the panels."

"Never mind," Mason said, "there's a woman in danger on the other side of that door. Smash it down."

Drake grabbed him and pulled him to one side. "Don't be a fool, Perry. I've seen too many of these things. We've trapped a killer in the kitchen. Telephone for the police. Use your head, and above all don't stand in front of those panels. When the killer knows he's trapped, there'll be a fusillade of bullets coming through there."

Mason stood contemplating the door, said, "All right, Paul. Telephone the police. I'll take a look at this man and see how long he's been dead."

The lawyer moved a step or two, then suddenly and unexpectedly hurled himself again at the kitchen door.

Once more the door yielded slightly, then pushed back shut.

Mason said, "Wait a minute, Paul. There's no one holding this door shut.

It's a chair or something propped against it and cushioned on some rubber so it — Come on, give me a hand here.''

''Just a minute,'' Drake said. ''I've got the police.''

The detective gave the address and number of the apartment, announced a dead man was on the floor, that the murderer or murderers were in the kitchen; that evidently they had the young woman who rented the apartment held as a hostage.

Drake hung up the phone.

Mason picked up a chair, swung it around in a circle and crashed it against the panels of the kitchen door.

The door panels splintered. Mason kicked some of the splinters away with his heel, looked inside the kitchen and said, ''A big kitchen table against the door and mattresses jammed between the wall and the table.''

''They're in the kitchen, I tell you,'' Drake said. ''Get away — the police will be here within a matter of seconds.''

Mason swung the chair again, crashed

another panel in the door, ripped out the panel with his bare hands, looked through the wrecked door into the kitchen, then suddenly turned and sprinted for the corridor.

"What's the matter?" Drake asked.

"There's a back door," Mason said. "It's open."

The lawyer reached the corridor, rounded a turn, went down an L in the corridor, came to an open door and entered the kitchen. Drake was a few steps behind him.

"Well," Drake said, "we certainly fell for that one. It felt just as though someone was holding that door. You can see what happened. They took two mattresses, put one between the table and the door, the other between the table and the electric stove. It would give just an inch or two but not enough to get the door open. It felt as if someone was holding it from the inside."

Drake ran back to the telephone, again called police, said, "Get your dispatcher to alert the cars coming in on that murder and kidnaping charge that at least one man and a woman — the woman probably being a hostage — have just made their escape from the apartment house. They may have reached the street but they can't have gone far. The radio car should be on the alert.''

Drake hung up the phone, then went over to where Mason was kneeling by the motionless figure on the floor.

''This guy's still alive,'' the lawyer said.

Drake felt for the man's pulse. ''Faint and thready,'' he said, ''but it's there. Guess we'd better phone for an ambulance. Oh-oh, look here.''

The detective indicated a small red stain on the front of the man's shirt.

He opened the shirt, pulled down the undershirt and disclosed a small puncture in the skin.

''What the deuce?'' Drake asked.

''The hole made by a twenty-two caliber bullet,'' Mason said. ''Let's be careful not to touch anything, Paul . . . . Get on that phone and tell the police that this man is still alive. Let's see if we can get an ambulance to rush him to the hospital,''

Again Drake went to the phone and put through the call. Then the lawyer and the detective stood for a few moments in the doorway.

''Where did those mattresses come from?'' Drake asked.

''Apparently off the twin beds in the bedroom,'' Mason said. ''They were taken to the kitchen. Evidently the idea was they would barricade themselves and shoot it out, and then they found they could close off the kitchen door and give themselves a chance to slip out into the corridor and down the stairs.''

''You think there were two?''

''There were two mattresses,'' Mason said. ''Evidently from the way the bedclothes are arranged, someone simply took hold of the ends of the mattresses and dragged them across the room. There probably wasn't time to make two trips, so there must have been at least two people or perhaps three people, because one of them must have been holding the girl — and that accounts for the scream we heard which was stifled.''

''They had to work fast from the time we first rang the chimes,'' Drake said. ''Of course we could hear the sound of people moving. It must have been —''

''It was probably all of fifteen seconds,'' Mason said. ''A lot could have been done in fifteen seconds. If that girl had only screamed earlier, we'd have been smashing our way in instead of standing there at the door like a couple of nitwits.''

''And the girl?'' Drake asked.

''My client, Dorrie Ambler,'' Mason said.

''You wouldn't think they could have gone far,'' Drake protested. ''They —''

A voice from the doorway said, ''What's going on here?''

Mason turned to the uniformed officer. ''Evidently there's been a shooting, a kidnaping and burglary. We trapped the people in the kitchen but they barricaded the kitchen door and got out through the service door.''

The officer moved over to the man on the floor, said, ''Looks to me as though

99

he'll be another D.O.A.''

''We have an ambulance coming,'' Mason said.

''So I've been advised. You have any description of the people who were in on this caper?''

Mason shook his head, said, ''I notified the polilce to have the dispatcher —''

''I know, I know,'' the officer said. ''We've got four radio cars converging on the district and they're stopping everyone coming out of the apartment house. But it's probably too late to do anything.

''Here's the ambulance now,'' he said, as they heard the sound of the siren.

The officer said, ''Okay, you fellows have done everything you can here. Now let's get back out in the corridor where we don't leave any more fingerprints than necessary. Let's try and keep all the evidence from being obliterated.''

Mason and Drake waited in the corridor until stretcher-bearers had taken the man from the room, until more police arrived, and then finally Lt. Tragg of Homicide.

"Well, well, well!" Tragg said. "This is an unusual experience. Usually you're on the other side of the fence, Perry. I understand now you've asked for police co-operation."

"I sure did," Mason told him. "I could now use a little of that police efficiency which has proven so embarrassing in times past."

"What can you tell us about the case?" Tragg asked.

"Nothing very much, I'm afraid," Mason said. "The occupant of this apartment consulted me in connection with a matter that I'm not at liberty to disclose at the moment, but she had reason to believe her personal safety might be jeopardized when she called me this morning."

"What time?"

"About twenty minutes past ten."

"How do you fix the time?"

"By other matters and by recollection."

"What other matters?"

101

"A court hearing in which I was interested, and which I was having covered."

"Playing it just a bit cozy, aren't you, Perry?" Tragg asked.

"I'm trying to do what's best for my client," Mason said. "I'm aware of the fact that communications made to the police quite frequently result in newspaper publicity and I'm not at all certain that my client would care to have any publicity concerning those matters. However, she did telephone me this morning and told me that she would like to have me come here at once, that she felt her apartment was being placed under surveillance by people who might have plans for her which she didn't like."

"And you and Paul Drake here constituted yourselves a bodyguard and came storming out to the scene," Tragg said. "Why didn't you telephone the police?"

"I don't think she wanted the police notified."

"What makes you think so?"

"She could have called them very easily and very handily if she had."

Tragg said, "There's a garage which goes with this building and we're going down and take a look in it. I think you and Drake had better come along with us. I don't like to leave you out of my sight."

"What about the stuff in there?" Mason asked, indicating the apartment.

"All that can wait," Tragg said. "Things are being guarded and whatever clues are there will be preserved, but I want to take a look at the garage and see what we find."

"You won't find anything," Mason said.

"What makes you think so?"

"Well, I feel that you *probably* won't find anything."

"You think the young woman was kidnaped in her car?"

"I don't know."

"But you do think she was kidnaped."

"I certainly think she was abducted against her will."

103

"Well, let's take a look," Tragg said. "I have some news for you, Perry."

"What?"

"The apartments in this building have private garages that are rented with the apartments. Our boys looked in the private garage that goes with this apartment and guess what they found?"

"Not the body of Miss Ambler?" Mason said.

"No, no, no," Tragg interposed hastily. "I didn't want to alarm you, Perry. I was trying to break it to you gently, however. We found something we've been looking for for a few days now."

"What?"

"We've been looking for a hit-and-run automobile, a light-colored Cadillac, license number WHW 694 that had been stolen from San Francisco on the fifth of September and was involved in a hit-and-run accident here on the sixth of September."

"You mean that car was in the garage?"

"That's right. Stolen automobile,

slight dent in the fender, broken left headlight lens — a perfect match for a jagged bit of broken headlight that was picked up at the scene of the accident. I'd like to have you take a look.''

"Then she was right," Mason said.

"Who was right?"

"My client."

"In what?"

"I don't think I can give you all the details at the moment, Tragg, but I may say that the presence of this automobile ties in with the reason she came to see me in the first place.''

"Very, very nice," Tragg said. "Now, if you want to help your client and help the police find her before something very serious happens to her, you can tell me a little bit more about just what it was she was worried about.''

"All right, I'll tell you this much," Mason said. "She had the distinct feeling that an attempt was going to be made to tie her in with that — Well, she felt it would be with *something* that happened on the sixth of September. She

105

didn't know for sure what it was.''

''And you took it on yourself to find out?''

''I did a little investigating.''

''And learned about the hit-and-run?''

''Yes.''

''And you knew the car that was involved in the hit-and-run was in this garage?''

''I certainly did not,'' Mason said, ''and for your information I haven't been an accessory after the fact on any hit-and-run, I haven't been covering up any crime, and that car was put in the garage a few minutes ago as part of this thing we're investigating.''

An officer came up in the elevator, handed Tragg a folded piece of paper.

Tragg opened it, read the message, folded the paper again, put it in his pocket, glanced at Perry Mason and said, ''Well, you can see what it feels like on the other side now, Perry.''

''What do you mean?''

''The man who was removed in the ambulance was dead on arrival, so now we have a homicide.''

"Let's hope we don't have two of them," Mason said.

Tragg led the way to the elevator, down to the basement floor, out into a parking place in the rear where there were rows of numbered garages.

"This way," Tragg said, leading the way across the parking place to the garage which bore the figure 907 above it.

Tragg took a key from his pocket, unlocked a padlock, said, "Now, I'm going to have to ask you to keep your hands in your pockets, not to touch a thing, I just want you to take a look, that's all."

Mason pushed his hands in his pockets. After a moment Drake followed suit.

Tragg switched on a light.

"There's the car," he said.

Mason looked at the big light-colored automobile.

"What about it?" he said.

Tragg said, "Take a look at that right-hand fender, Perry. Stand over this way a little bit — a little farther — right

107

here. See it? See the spider web and the flies in it? The spider web goes from the emblem on the car to the edge of the little tool bench in the garage, and notice the flies that are in it. That spider web has been there for some time."

Tragg, watching Mason's face, said, "I've been in this business, Perry, long enough to know that you can't trust a woman when she's telling a story, particularly if she's had an opportunity to rehearse that story.

"If Dorrie Ambler is your client, she may or may not have been abducted. There was a murdered man on the floor of her apartment. She may or may not have been responsible for that, but there's an automobile in her garage and she sure as hell is responsible for that automobile. That's a stolen automobile in the first place, and in the second place it was involved in a hit-and-run.

"Now then, Perry, I'm going to ask you just how much do you know about Dorrie Ambler?"

Mason was thoughtfully silent for a moment, then said, "Not too much."

"Everything based on what she's told you?"

"Everything based on what she's told me," Mason said.

"All right," Tragg said. "I'm not going to tell anybody that I showed you that spider web. We're going to have it sprayed and photographed. It'll be a big point in the district attorney's case whenever the case comes up.

"I've shown you that on my own responsibility. I want to make a trade with you. That's information that's vital to your client. I think you have some information that's vital to me."

Tragg ushered Mason and the detective from the garage, locked the door behind them.

"How about it, Perry?" he asked.

Mason said, "Tragg, I'd like to co-operate with you but I'm going to have to think things over a bit and I'm going to have to do some checking on certain information."

"And after you've checked on it you'll give us everything you can?"

"Everything I feel that I can

conscientiously give you and which will be to the advantage of my client, I will.''

''All right,'' Tragg said, ''if that's the best you can do, that's what we'll have to take.''

''And,'' Mason said, ''I'd like to ask one thing of you.''

''What?''

''As soon as you get in touch with my client, will you let me know?''

''When we get in touch with your client, Mason, we'll be questioning her in regard to a murder and a hit-and-run and we'll tell her she has an opportunity to consult counsel if she desires, but we're going to do everything in the world to make her talk. You know that.''.

''Yes,'' Mason said, ''I know that.''

Chapter Six

Mason turned to Drake as soon as Tragg was out of earshot and said, "Get your office, Paul. I want Minerva Minden. I want to talk with her before the police do."

"Okay," Drake said, "we'd better go down the street a ways before we do any telephoning."

Mason said, "She may still be at the courthouse."

"Could be," Drake said, "but I have an idea her lawyer whisked her out of circulation just as rapidly as possible.

"You know and I know that a thousand-dollar fine means no more to Minerva Minden than the nickel she dropped into the parking meter. The tongue-lashing given her by the judge

111

was just so much sound as far as Minny Minden was concerned. That girl has been in enough scrapes to learn how to roll with the punch. She listened demurely to the judge's lecture, paid the thousand dollars with due humility and then looked for some place where she could open a bottle of champagne and celebrate her victory.

"Judges don't like to have persons who have been sentenced by them celebrating. Attorneys know that, and the attorney is thinking not only about this case but about Minny's next one and about his next one before that same judge, so my best guess is he's told her to get out of circulation, stay away from the public, see no one and refuse to come to the telephone."

"That," Mason said, "makes sense. That's what I'd do under the circumstances if she were my client, Paul. However, let's go phone your office and see what the reports are."

They drove half a dozen blocks before Mason found a gasoline station with a telephone booth which seemed

112

sufficiently removed from the scene of operations.

Drake put through the call, came back and said, "Everything checks, Perry. She was whisked away from the courthouse by her attorney. She went into the telephone booth to make some jubilee calls, but he caught up with her after the first two and dragged her out of there. He put her in his car and personally drove her to Montrose. Presumably they're both there now."

"Who's her attorney?" Mason asked.

"Herbert Knox," Drake said, "of Gambit, Knox & Belam."

"Old Herb Knox, huh?" Mason said. "He's a smooth article. Tell me, did he act as her attorney when she received her inheritance?"

"I don't know," Drake said, "but I don't think so. As I remember it she's done a little shopping around with attorneys."

"Well, she couldn't have had a better one than Herbert Knox for this particular job," Mason said. "He's smooth and suave and a wily veteran of the courtroom.''

''All right, what do we do now?'' Drake said.

Mason thought for a moment, then said, ''We get busy on the telephone. Let's call Minerva at her place in Montrose and see what we can get.''

''It'll be an unlisted number,'' Drake said.

Mason shook his head. ''They'll have two or three telephones, Paul. Two of them will be unlisted but there'll be one telephone that's listed. That will be answered by a secretary or a business manager but we can at least use it to get a message through to her.''

''Will getting a message through do any good?'' Drake asked.

''I think it will,'' Mason said. ''I think I can convey a message which will make her sit up and take notice.''

Drake, who had been looking through the telephone book, said, ''Okay, here's the number. You were right. There's a listed telephone.''

Mason put through the call and heard a well-modulated feminine voice saying,

"May I help you? This is the Minden residence."

"This is Perry Mason, the attorney," Mason said. "I want to talk with Miss Minden."

"I'm afraid that's impossible, Mr. Mason, but I might be able to take a message."

"Tell her," Mason said, "that I know who fired the shots at the airport and that I want to talk with her about it."

"I'll convey that message to her. And where can I communicate with you, Mr. Mason?"

"I'll hang on the line."

"I'm sorry, that's not possible. I can't reach her that soon."

"Why not? Isn't she there?" Mason asked.

"I'll call you later at your office. Thank you," the feminine voice said, and the connection clicked.

Mason said, "Paul, there's just a chance we can get out to her place at Montrose before Herbert Knox leaves. If I can talk with her, I may be able to clear up certain things and we may be able to get some information that will save Dorrie Ambler's life. I don't want to tell the police all that I know but I have a feeling that — Come on, Paul, let's go."

"On our way," Drake said, "but I'll bet you old Herb Knox won't let you get within a mile of his client."

"Don't bet too much," Mason said. "You may lose."

They made good time over the freeways which at this time of the day were free of congestion and handling a stream of swiftly moving traffic which was a trickle compared to the masses of cars that would crowd through during the afternoon rush hour.

The Montrose estate of Minerva Minden was an imposing edifice on a hill, and Mason, driving up the sweeping graveled driveway through the beautifully landscaped grounds, swung his car into a parking place which contained an even dozen automobiles.

"Looks like there might be a lot of other people with the same idea," Drake said.

"Probably some of them are reporters, some are employees," Mason said. "You don't know what kind of a car Herbert Knox drives, do you, Paul?"

"No."

"I have an idea one of these cars may be his. I hope so."

The men parked their car, went up the stairs to the broad porch. Mason rang the bell.

A burly individual who looked more like a bodyguard than a butler opened the door and stood silent.

"I would like to see Minerva Minden's confidential secretary or business manager," Mason said. "I am Perry Mason and I'm calling in connection with an emergency."

The man said, "Wait here," turned to a telephone in the wall and relayed a message into a mouthpiece so constructed that it was impossible for bystanders to hear what was being said.

After a moment, he said, "Who's the gentleman with you?"

"Paul Drake, a private detective."

Again the man turned to the phone,

then after a moment hung up and said, "This way, please."

Mason and Drake entered a reception hallway, and followed the butler into a room which had at one time evidently been a library. Now it was fixed up as a sort of intermediate waiting room with a table, rugs, indirect lighting, deep leather-cushioned chairs and an atmosphere which combined that of a luxurious room in an expensive residence with that of an office where people waited.

"Be seated, please," the butler said, and left the room.

A moment later a tall, keen-eyed woman in her late forties or early fifties entered the room and strode directly across to Mason. "How do you do, Mr. Mason," she said. "I am Henrietta Hull, Miss Minden's confidential secretary and manager; and this, I presume, is Mr. Paul Drake, the detective."

She moved easily to a chair, regarded the men with keen, appraising eyes for a moment, then said, "You wished to see

118

me, Mr. Mason?"

"Actually," Mason said, "I want to see Minerva Minden."

"Many people do," Henrietta Hull said.

Mason smiled. "Is it Miss Hull or Mrs. Hull?"

"It's Henrietta Hull," the woman said, smiling, "but if you *need* any other handle, it's Mrs."

"Would it be possible for us to see Miss Minden?"

"It would be utterly impossible, Mr. Mason. Nothing, absolutely nothing, that you could say would gain you an audience. In fact I may go a little further and state that when Miss Minden's attorney learned that you were seeking an interview, he gave Miss Minden particular instructions that under no circumstances was she to talk with you."

"I'll talk with him if I have to," Mason said.

Henrietta Hull shook her head. "That would do no good, Mr. Mason. Mr. Knox is not Miss Minden's regular attorney.''

''Who is?'' Mason asked.

''There isn't any,'' Henrietta Hull said. ''Miss Minden retains counsel as she needs them. She tries to get the very best in the field. For a matter of this sort Herbert Knox was considered the best available attorney.''

''May I ask why?'' Mason asked.

Her eyes softened somewhat. ''You're asking because you feel professionally slighted?'' she asked.

''No,'' Mason said, ''I was just wondering. You seemed so positive. I gathered that you keep some sort of list of attorneys.''

''We do, Mr. Mason,'' she said, ''and you might be interested to know that you head the list of attorneys available in murder cases or serious felonies. There are other attorneys who are selected for their ability in connection with automobile cases and traffic violations. Mr. Knox was selected in this case because of various qualifications, not the least of which is that he is frequently a golfing partner of the judge before whom the case was tried.''

''And how,'' Mason asked, ''did you know the particular judge who would be assigned to the case?''

She smiled and said, ''After all, Mr. Mason, you had a matter you wanted to take up with Miss Minden.''

''All right,'' Mason said, ''I'll put my cards on the table. Miss Minden has hired a double.''

''Indeed?'' Henrietta Hull said, her eyebrows raising. ''You're making a positive statement, Mr. Mason?''

''I'm making a positive statement.''

''All right,'' Henrietta Hull said. ''Your statement is that she hired a double. Now what?''

Mason said, ''The disturbance at the airport was shrewdly engineered to bring out the fact that Miss Minden had a double, but Miss Minden did some very fast and some very shrewd thinking and decided it would be better for her to take the responsibility of firing the shots than to expose the fact that she had hired a double.''

''This is rather a startling statement,

Mr. Mason. I trust you have evidence to back up your statement.''

''I am making a statement,'' Mason said. ''I would like to have you convey it to Minerva Minden. I would also like to have you tell her that I can be rather a ruthless antagonist, that I don't know *all* the ramifications of the game she is playing but that I rather suspect the ad by which this double was chosen — or rather the ad which served as bait to bring this double into the position that had been selected for her — was shrewdly designed as the elaborate bait in a deadly trap.

''I don't know whether Minerva Minden knew that this double of hers was going to be placed in a position of danger or not, but a situation has now developed where that young woman is in very great danger. I have been invited to tell the police what I know. I don't want to release a story which may result in a lot of newspaper notoriety for Miss Minden.''

Henrietta Hull smiled and said, ''Miss Minden is not a stranger to newspaper notoriety.''

''You mean she enjoys it?'' Mason asked sharply.

''I mean that she is not a stranger to it.''

''All right,'' Mason said. ''I think I've told you enough so that you can appreciate my position and the fact it is imperative I have an immediate interview with Miss Minden.''

''An immediate interview is out of the question,'' Henrietta Hull said. ''But, as I told you over the telephone, Mr. Mason, I will be glad to convey a message and to call you at your office.''

''When?'' Mason asked.

''As soon as necessary arrangements have been made or perhaps I should say as soon as necessary precautions have been taken.

''All right,'' Mason said. ''I just want to point out to you that traffic violations are one thing, firing blank cartridges is another thing. But kidnaping is a felony that carries very serious penalties, and murder is punishable by death.''

''Thank you, Mr. Mason,'' Henrietta

Hull said. "Of course you're an attorney, but as a business woman I am familiar with certain phases of the law."

She arose abruptly, signifying that the interview was terminated. She gave Mason her hand and the benefit of a long, steady appraisal. Then she turned to Paul Drake. "I'm very pleased to have met you, Mr. Drake. I may also advise you that your agency is at the top of the list which we maintain in cases where a highly ethical agency is required."

Drake smiled. "Meaning that you have a list of unethical agencies?"

"We have very complete lists," she said enigmatically. Then again turned to Mason. "And don't forget, Mr. Mason, that your name is absolute tops in cases carrying a serious penalty."

"Such as murder?" Mason asked.

"Such as murder," Henrietta Hull said, and then after a moment added, "and such as kidnaping or abduction."

Chapter Seven

Mason fitted his latchkey to the door of his private office, entered and was confronted by Della Street, who said, "Why secretaries get gray. . . . Do you realize, Mr. Perry Mason, that you have two appointments I've had to stall off and if it hadn't been for the noon hour intervening you'd have had more. I told them that you were out at a luncheon club making a speech."

"You're getting to be a pretty good extemporaneous prevaricator," Mason said.

She smiled. "Freely translated that means I'm a graceful, gifted, talented offhand liar. . . . You see what you've done to my morals, Mr. Perry Mason."

"The constant dripping of water,"

Mason said, "can wear away the toughest stone."

"We were talking about morals, I believe. I suppose there was some major emergency."

"There was a very great major emergency."

"Have you had lunch?"

"No."

"You have some appointments that I've been stalling off. I told them you'd see them right after lunch and then told them that you were delayed getting back from lunch."

"They're in the outer office?"

"Yes."

"What else?" Mason asked.

"I believe you are acquainted with a very firm and dignified young woman named Henrietta Hull who is the secretary to Minerva Minden?"

"She isn't young," Mason said. "She has a sense of humor. She puts up a good front of being firm. What about her?"

"She called up, said that she was to leave a message for you, that she was sorry that there was no possiblity of your seeing Miss Minden; that you might care to know, however, that Dorrie Ambler had been followed by a detective agency employed by Miss Minden ever since Miss Ambler had attempted to blackmail Miss Minden into making a property settlement on her."

"What else?" Mason asked.

"That was all," she said. "She told me that perhaps you should have that information."

"I'll be damned," Mason said.

"And," Della Street went on, "Jerry Nelson, Drake's operative, said he missed you at the place he was told to report. He said Drake was out so he came down here to tell me that there's a difference in coloring between Dorrie Ambler and Minerva Minden but aside from that the resemblance is startling. He said it might be very easy for an eyewitness to confuse one with the other."

"But there was a discernible difference?"

"Oh, yes. He felt *he* could tell one

from the other.''

''By what means? Just what is the difference?''

''Well, he couldn't put his finger on it. He said that it's something — He thinks the hair may be a little different and something about the complexion, but he says there's a resemblance that — Well, the only way that he could describe it was to say it was startling.''

Mason's unlisted phone rang.

''That's Paul Drake,' Mason said, and picked up the receiver.

Paul Drake's voice came over the line. ''I'm sorry to bring you bad news, Perry.''

''What?'

''We were followed out to Minerva Minden's .''

''How do you know?''

''I found out when I was parking the car.''

''How do you mean?''

''They have a plug they can slip on the end of the exhaust pipe. It releases drops of fluorescent liquid at regular intervals. By wearing a certain type of spectacles with lenses that are tinted so it can make these drops visible, they can follow a car even if they're ten or fifteen minutes behind it.''

''And you know your car was fixed?''

''It was fixed all right.''

''But you don't know that they followed us.''

''I don't *know* they followed us,'' Drake said, ''but knowing Tragg as I do, I know he wasn't wasting the taxpayers' equipment just for the sake of the exercise.''

''Thanks, Paul,'' Mason said. ''I have an office full of irate clients and I've got to get down to a little routine work, but you get busy and see what you can find out.''

''We're already busy,'' Drake said. ''I've got tentacles stretching out in every direction, trying to cover eveything I can.''

''What about the kidnapping, Paul?''

''I don't know. The police are playing it awfully close to their chest. Of course, under the circumstances you can realize that they wouldn't take us into their confidence, and it's probably good business not to tell the newspapers too much about it, but they're certainly playing it cozy.''

"All right," Mason said, "you get busy, Paul, and find out everything you can. Try particularly to find out something about the background of Dorrie Ambler.''

"You don't think you should tell the police what you know?''

"I'm hanged if I know, Paul," Mason said. "I think probably I will, but I want to think it over a bit. I'll get rid of a few pressing appointments and then be in touch with you.''

"Okay," Drake said, "I'll be on the job.''

Mason said to Della Street, "I guess I'll copy Paul Drake's diet, Della. Get me a couple of sandwiches from the restaurant around the corner and put some coffee on. I'll start seeing these clients who have been waiting .''

"Don't you want to wait and eat afterwards?'' Della Street asked.

"Frankly I do," Mason said, "but

some of those clients are a little angry. They feel they've been cooling their heels in my outer office while I've been out to lunch, enjoying myself.

"The psychological effect of having a hamburger sandwich in one hand and a lawbook in the other is remarkably soothing to the irate client. I'll tell them I had such an important matter come up I had to break my luncheon engagement."

"In other words," Della Street said, "these sandwiches are to be props."

"Props with a use," Mason said. "Send in the first client, Della, and go get the sandwiches as soon as he comes in."

She glided out into the outer office and a moment later Mason's first client stalking into the room.

Mason said, "I'm sorry I had to keep you waiting. I was out on a major emergency. I'm going to impose on your good nature by grabbing a sandwich while we talk. I'm famished.

"Della, hand me that file with the memorandum on this case and get a couple of hamburgers, if you will.''

"Right away,'' Della Street promised, handling him the filing jacket.

As Mason opened the folder the expression on the client's face softened.

Mason hurried through that interview and four more, nibbling at sandwiches and drinking coffee.

He was interviewing his last client when the telephone rang three short bells signaling that the switchboard operator was holding an important call.

Della Street picked up the telephone, said, ''Yes, Gertie,'' then turned to Mason. ''Lieutenant Tragg,'' she said.

''In the office?'' Mason asked.

''No, on the line.''

Mason picked up the telephone, said, ''Yes, Lieutenant, this is Mason.''

Tragg said, ''I've given you some breaks today, Mason. I'm going to give you some more.''

''Yes,'' Mason said dryly. ''I hope the substance you put on the exhaust of my automobile doesn't interfere with the operating efficiency.''

''Oh, not at all, not at all,''

Tragg said.

"I presume my car was followed," Mason observed.

"Oh, of course," Tragg said casually. "You wouldn't expect us to have you right in our hands, so to speak, and then let you slip through our fingers. We know all about your trip out to Miss Minden's at Montrose."

"I presume," Mason said, "you're going to extend some more favors and I'll find that they were simply bait for a very elaborate trap."

"Oh, but such beautiful bait," Tragg said. "This is something that you absolutely can't resist, Perry."

"What is it?" Mason asked.

Tragg said, "I felt that you couldn't make time enough to get here so I'm sending an officer. He should be in your office within a matter of seconds. If you and Della Street will come up here — just walk right into my office in case I shouldn't be there. If I'm not in, I won't keep you waiting very long. I'll really do you a favor."

"Bait?" Mason asked.

"Beautiful bait," Tragg said, and hung up.

Again the phone rang, a series of short, sharp rings. Della Street picked it up, said, "Yes, Gertie?" Then turned to Mason. "A uniformed officer is in the outer office. He has a police car down in front with the motor running and instructions to get both of us to Headquarters just as fast as possible."

Mason's client jumped up. "Well, I think we've covered most of the points, Counselor. Thank you. I'll get in touch with you."

Mason said, "Sorry," pushed back his chair, cupped his hand over Della Street's elbow, said, "Come on, Della, let's go."

"You think it's that important?" Della Street asked.

Mason said, "At this stage of the case I welcome any new developments, either pro or con. . . . Remember, Della, no talking in the police car. Those officers sometimes have big ears."

Della Street nodded.

They hurried out to the outer office.

The waiting officer said, "I'm under instructions to get you to Headquarters just as fast as possible without using red light or siren, but hogging traffic all the way."

"All right," Mason told him, "let's hog traffic."

They hurried to the elevator. The officer escorted them to a curb where another officer was sitting behind the wheel of a police automobile, the motor running.

Perry Mason held the rear door open for Della Street, assisted her in, jumped in beside her and almost immediately the car whipped out into traffic.

"Good heavens," Della Street said under her breath as they went through the first intersection.

"It's their business," Mason told her reassuringly. "They drive in traffic all the time and they're in a hurry."

"I'll say they're in a hurry," Della Street said.

The car wove its way through traffic, crowded signals; twice the driver turned on the red light. Once he gave a light tap on the button of the siren. Aside from that they used no official prerogatives except the skill born of long practice and a deft, daring technique.

There had been no need for Mason's admonition about conversation. The occupants of the automobile had been far too busy to engage in any small talk. As the car glided in to the reserved parking place at Police Headquarters, the driver said, "Just take that elevator to the third floor. Tragg's office."

"I know," Mason said.

The elevator operator was waiting for them. As they entered, the door was slammed shut and they were taken directly to the third floor without intermediate stops.

Mason exchanged a meaningful glance with Della Street.

As the operator came to a stop they left the elevator, crossed the corridor and opened the door to Tragg's office.

A uniformed officer sitting at the desk jerked his thumb toward the inner office. "Go right on in," he said.

"Tragg there?" Mason asked.

"He said for you to go in," the officer said.

Mason crossed over to the door, held it open for Della Street, then followed her into the room and came to an abrupt stop.

"Good heavens, Miss Ambler," he said, "you certainly had me worried. Can you tell me what happened to —"

Della Street tugged at Mason's coat.

The young woman who sat in the chair on the far side of Lt. Tragg's desk swept Mason with cool, appraising eyes, then said in a deep, throaty voice, "Mr. Mason, I presume, and I suppose this young woman with you is your secretary I've heard so much about?"

Mason bowed. "Miss Della Street."

"I'm Minerva Minden," she said. "You've been trying to see me and I didn't want to see you. I didn't know that you had enough pull with the police department to arrange an interview under circumstances of this sort."

"I didn't either," Mason said.

"However," she said, "the results seem to speak for themselves."

Mason said, "Actually, Miss Minden, I didn't have any idea that *you* would be here. Lieutenant Tragg called me and asked me to come to his office. He said that if he wasn't in we were to go to the private office and wait. I assume that he intends to interview us together."

"I would assume so," she said, in the same low, throaty voice.

"All right," Mason said, turning to Della Street, "is this the woman who was in our office, Della?"

Della Street shook her head. "There are some things that only a woman would notice," she said, "but it's not the same one."

"All right," Mason said, turning to Minerva Minden, "but there's a startling resemblance."

"I am quite familiar with the resemblance," she said. "In case you're interested, Mr. Mason, it has been used to try and blackmail me."

"What do you mean?"

"I mean that Dorrie Ambler feels that she is related to the relative from whom I received a large inheritance. She has been importuning me to make her a very substantial cash settlement and when I told her I wouldn't do anything of the sort, she threatened to put me in such a position that I'd find myself on the defensive and would be only too glad to — as she put it — pay through the nose in order to get out."

"You've seen her?" Mason asked.

"I haven't met her personally but I've talked with her on the telephone and I have — Well, frankly, I've had detectives on her trail."

"For how long?"

"I don't think I care to answer that question, Mr. Mason."

"All right," Mason said, "that's not the story I heard."

"I'm satisfied it isn't," she said. "I'm satisfied that Dorrie Ambler, who apparently is a remarkably intelligent and ingenious young woman, and who is being masterminded by a very clever manager, has arranged a series of circumstances so that she would have a very convincing background against which to reassert her claims.

"I may tell you, Mr. Mason, that that stunt she pulled following me to the airport, of getting clothes that were the exact duplicates of the clothes I had, of waiting until I had gone to the rest room, then firing a revolver loaded with blank cartridges and dashing into the rest room, jumping into the shower compartment and closing the door, was a remarkably ingenious bit of work.

"If I hadn't kept my head I would have found myself in quite a sorry situation."

"Just how?" Mason asked.

"Well, naturally," Minerva Minden said, "being in a cubicle behind a closed door I wasn't entirely conversant with what had happened. However, when I went out and was immediately identified by bystanders as the woman who had caused the commotion, I did some mighty quick thinking and realized what must have happened."

"And so?" Mason asked.

"So," she said, "I took it in my stride. Instead of insisting that there was a mistake and getting the officers to have a policewoman search the rest room, and have Dorrie Ambler claim, when she was brought out, that *I* was the one who had fired shots, thus giving the newspapers a field day; and instead of giving Dorrie the chance to insist in public that our rather striking resemblance was due to common ancestors, I simply accepted the responsibility and permitted myself to be taken to the station. There I was booked on charges of disturbing the peace and discharging a firearm within the city limits and in a public place.''

''You're lucky that's all of the charges that were made against you,'' Mason said.

''Yes,'' she said, ''Dorrie was considerate there. I misunderstood the witness for a moment, or rather I think they all misunderstood Dorrie. She evidently said 'This is *not* a stick-up,' but when the witnesses identified me, two of them said that I had brandished a gun and said 'This *is* a stick-up' and I didn't deny it until afterwards, when I had my hearing in court this morning.

By that time my attorney had unearthed witnesses who had heard what was said and remembered it accurately. I think that was one of the big facts in my favor."

Mason said, "I'm going to put it right up to you fairly and frankly: Did you put an ad in the paper asking for a young woman who —"

"Oh, bosh and nonsense, Mr. Mason,' she said. "Don't be a sap. Dorrie Ambler put that ad in the paper herself. Then she went out and got a detective agency to front in the case. She would give them instructions over the telephone at an unlisted number and had everything all arranged so that quite naturally she would be the one who was selected for the job. It was an elaborate job of window-dressing."

"And the detective agency will then defeat it all by showing that she was the person who was back of it all?"

"The detective agency is not in a position to do any such thing," she said. "I've tried to uncover it without any success. The detective agency simply knows that they were hired on a cash basis to screen applicants; that they were given photographs and told that whenever any woman bore a really striking resemblance to those photographs she was to be tentatively hired.''

''And the photographs were of you?'' Mason asked.

''The photographs were *not* of me,'' she said, ''although they might well have been. Actually, and that is where Dorrie Ambler made a fatal mistake, she couldn't get photographs of me so she had to use some of herself. While I have had many news photographs taken, she wanted portrait photos of front and side views and she had to have them in a hurry.

''It would have attracted attention if a woman who looked so much like me had either solicited photographs of me or tried to get someone else to procure them. It was much more simple to go to a photographer and have the shots taken that she wanted.''

''All of this must have taken a certain

amount of money,'' Mason said.

''Of course it took a certain amount of money,'' she said. ''I don't know who's financing her, but I have an idea it's some very crooked, very clever Las Vegas businessman.

''And furthurmore, I don't think Dorrie Ambler entered the picture under her own power, so to speak. I think that this confidence man or promoter got to nosing around and found her in Nevada and got her to come here and take this apartment, to settle down here just as if she were an average young woman planning on living here. Then instead of coming out and trying to make a claim against the money I had inherited and putting herself in a position where *she'd* be carrying the burden of proof, they were smart enough to think up a whole series of situations in which I would be the one that was on the defensive and it would suit the convenience of the newspapers to play up the startling resemblance. That would get her case against me off to a flying start.''

''The hit-and-run?'' Mason asked.

"I'm not prepared to say about the hit-and-run," Minerva said. "That may have been accidental. But she *was* teamed up with crooks. You know that because the car was stolen."

"It was her idea," Mason said dryly, "that perhaps *you'd* been the one to hit this man in the hit-and-run accident and had used her as a cover-up."

Minerva Minden laughed. "Now, isn't that a likely story," she said. "Don't tell me that *you* fell for that one, Mr. Mason.

"The pay-off, of course, is that the accident took place in a stolen car. I am not the possessor of a completely untarnished reputation, Mr. Mason. My driving record is fairly well studded with citations and I would dislike to have to acknowledge another traffic accident. However, I think you will agree that the idea that I would be driving a stolen car is just a little farfetched.

"And," Minerva Minden went on, "the man who was found fatally wounded in Dorrie Ambler's apartment was the detective who had assisted her in

145

putting her swindle across, a member of the firm of Billings and Compton. The dead man was Marvin Billings. His death will seal his lips so he can't testify against her. I make no accusations, but you must admit his death is quite fortunate.

"I'm not any plaster saint. I've been in lots of scrapes in my time and to be perfectly frank with you I expect to be in a lot more before I retire from active life. I want life, I want adventure, I want action, and I intend to get all three.

"I'm given to the unconventional in every sense of the word and in all of its various forms, but I am not given to stealing, I am not given to murder, and I don't have to use stolen cars to take me where I'm going."

Mason said, "Have you ever been operated on for appendicitis, Miss Minden?"

"Appendicitis? No, why?"

"This is very unconventional," the lawyer said, "but it happens to be important. Would you mind turning your back to me and letting Miss Street look to see if there's a scar on your abdomen?"

The girl laughed. "Why must I be so modest? Good heavens, you'd see that much of me in a Bikini. If you think it's important, take a look."

She got up, faced them, pulled up her blouse, loosened her skirt, slipped it far down and stretched out the skin over the place where a scar would have been.

"Satisfied?" she asked. "Feel the skin if you want."

Before Mason could answer, the door from the outer office burst open explosively, and Lt. Tragg hurried into the room.

"Well, well, well," he said, "what is this — a strip tease?"

Minerva Minden said, "Mr. Mason wanted to check to see if I had had an operation for appendicitis."

"I see," Tragg said. "Now that we're all here I'll ask your pardon for having kept you waiting. I want to ask a few questions."

"What questions do *you* want to ask?" Minerva Minden inquired, adjusting her clothing.

"In *your* case," Lt. Tragg said, "quite frankly, Miss Minden, I wanted to ask questions about a murder and you may be the prime suspect. I feel I should warn you."

"If you want to interrogate me about a murder case," she said, "and there's any possibility that I am going to be a suspect, I will have to ask you to interrogate my attorney and get your facts from him."

"And your attorney?" Tragg asked.

Minerva Minden turned to Perry Mason with a slow smile. "My attorney," she said, "is Mr. Perry Mason. I believe you were told by my secretary and manager, Henrietta Hull, Mr. Mason, that you were at the top of the list as potential counsel in the event of any serious charge being made against me."

Tragg turned to Mason. "You're representing her, Mason?"

"I am not," Mason said vehemently. "I'm representing Dorrie Ambler, and there's a very distinct conflict of interest. I couldn't represent Minerva Minden even if I wanted to."

"Now, that's not a very chivalrous attitude, Mr. Mason," Minerva said. "What's more, it's not a very good business attitude. I am perfectly willing to let you represent Miss Ambler in any way that you want to in connection with any claims to an inheritance, but I am quite certain Lieutenant Tragg will assure you that in case any murder charges are to be pressed against me —"

"I didn't say they *were*," Tragg said. "I said that I wanted to interrogate you in connection with a murder and that you *may* be a suspect."

"Whose murder?"

"The murder of Marvin Billings," Lt. Tragg said. "His partner says Billings was working for you at the time of his death, that he was going to interview Miss Dorrie Ambler at your request."

"And so I killed him — to keep him from following instructions?"

"I don't know," Tragg said. "I only wanted to question you ."

"You'll have to see my lawyer," she said. "I'm not going to talk with you until I've talked with him."

Tragg asked, "Do you know Marvin Billings, the man who was found in a dying condition on the floor of Miss Ambler's apartment?"

"The apartment is one that I know nothing about," she said firmly. "And I have never met Marvin Billings."

"The landlady identified your picture as being the one who lived in the apartment under the name of Dorrie Ambler, and she picked you out of a line-up."

Minerva Minden said casually, "Well, before she identifies me as Dorrie Ambler, you'd better have Dorrie Ambler in the line-up and *then* see who she identifies."

"I know, I know," Lt. Tragg said. "We're investigating, that's all. We're just trying to get the situation unscrambled."

"Well, if you ask me," Minerva Minden said, "this girl is a complete phony, a fraud an adventuress who has been trying to lay a foundation to present a claim against my uncle's estate.

"Evidently," Tragg said, "she knew nothing about her rights as a potential heiress."

"Phooey!" Miss Minden said. "She's already tried to shake me down for a settlement. That's what started this whole thing. Then she got plastered, clobbered a pedestrian and suddenly decided she'd kill two birds with one stone, getting me involved in a lot of publicity and — I'm not going to sit here and argue. I'm going to get up and walk out of here. If you want me for anything in the future, you can come out with a warrant for my arrest, and not ask for *me* to please come to Headquarters to help clarify things — and then run Perry Mason in on me.

"Now then, is this interview going to be kept confidential or not?"

"I'm afraid ," Lt. Tragg said, "that in matters which are subject to police investigation, we are not in a position to withhold facts from the public."

"And I presume," Mason said, "that you wanted to get a spontaneous identification from Miss Street and from me and for that reason you carefully arranged this so that we would walk in on Miss Minden and you would be in a position to hear our remarks."

"He wasn't in the room at the time," Minerva Minden said.

Mason smiled. "I am afraid you underestimate the police intelligence, Miss Minden. I take it, Lieutenant, that the room is bugged."

"Sure, it's bugged," Tragg said. "And you're quite right. I wanted to see your reaction when you first entered the room. Now, I take it there is a very strong resemblance between these two women, Dorrie Ambler and Minerva Minden."

"I don't think that I care to add anything to my comments at this time," Mason said. "I somewhat resent being dragged down here to make an identification for you."

"Oh, you weren't dragged," Tragg said. "You came of your own volition and you got something that you wanted very much — an opportunity to talk with Minerva Minden.''

''In other words you baited the trap with something that you thought I would fall for,'' Mason said.

''Of course, of course.'' Tragg beamed. ''We wouldn't bait a mouse trap with catnip and we wouldn't bait a cat trap with cheese.''

''*I* feel that *I* have been betrayed all the way along the line and that the police have abused their power,'' Minerva Minden said. She turned to Perry Mason. ''I wish you *would* agree to represent me, Mr. Mason — not on anything in connection with the estate, just this.''

Mason shook his head. ''I'm afraid there would be a conflict of interests.''

''Are you going to represent Dorrie Ambler in a claim against the estate?''

''I don't know. I haven't talked with her about that.''

Lt. Tragg said, ''Of course, Perry, I can begin to put two and two together now and I'd like very, very much to have you tell us the conversation you had with Miss Ambler. I think it might give us some clues — And what about the appendicitis scar?''

''I'm sorry,'' Mason said firmly, ''I don't feel that I'm in a position to make any disclosures.''

''All right,'' Tragg said, smiling, ''school's dismissed. Police cars are waiting to return you to your respective destinations.''

Minerva Minden stalked toward the door, suddenly whirled, came over to Perry Mason and extended her hand. ''I like you,'' she said.

''Thank you,'' Mason said.

''You won't reconsider about being my attorney?''

''No.''

Minerva smiled at Della Street, turned her back on Tragg and left the room.

''That was rather rough,'' Mason said to Tragg.

''It was, for a fact,'' Tragg said, ''but I had to find out for sure about the extent of the resemblance.''

''You're now satisfied that there's a

strong resemblance?'' Mason asked.

''I'm satisfied it's a striking resemblance,'' Tragg said. ''I notice that Della Street was watching her like a hawk. What did you think, Della?''

''Her hair isn't quite the same color,'' Della Street said. ''She doesn't use the same make-up, the tinting of the nails is different and — oh, there are quite a few little things that a woman would notice, but I can tell you the physical resemblance is really startling. The voices are the big difference. Dorrie Ambler talks rapidly and in a high-pitched voice.''

''Well, thanks a lot,'' Tragg said. ''I had to do it that way, Perry, because you wouldn't co-operate otherwise. The car will take you back to your office.''

Chapter Eight

Mason and Della dropped in at Paul Drake's office on the way back from Police Headquarters.

"Got a crying towel handy, Paul?" Mason asked.

"I always keep one in the upper right-hand drawer," Drake said.

"Get it out," Mason told him, "because you've lost a lucrative job."

"How come?"

"The police have moved in. I think the FBI may move in. They're considering the possibility of a kidnaping but the local police are still about two-thirds sold on the idea that Dorrie Ambler killed the detective who was trying to shake her down and then slipped out."

Drake said, "That sounds logical enough."

"Or she could have been defending herself when they tried to abduct her," Mason said.

"And killed a blackmailing detective?" Drake asked.

"Stranger things *have* happened," Mason pointed out.

"Name one," Drake said.

Mason grinned. He said, "For your information, I've now talked with Minerva Minden."

"She finally consented to see you?" Drake asked.

"Lieutenant Tragg arranged a trap," Mason said. "He sent for me to come up to his office on a very urgent matter. He insisted that Della Street come along. He had us shown into his office. Minerva was sitting there. I think Tragg wanted to see just how close the resemblance was between Minerva and Dorrie Ambler."

"How close was it?" Drake asked.

"So darned close that it had *me* fooled," Mason said. "Della Street saw

157

the difference.''

''I saw a difference in the little things that a woman would notice,'' Della Street said. ''The coloring, mostly.''

''The voices are quite different,'' Mason said, ''but in my opinion the resemblance simply can't be coincidental. I think when we find Dorrie Ambler we'll find another heir to the Harper Minden fortune.''

''And then there'll be a knock-down, drag-out fight between Minerva Minden and Dorrie Ambler?''

''That would be my guess,'' Mason said. ''You'll remember that Minerva Minden's mother had a sister who died, presumably without leaving any issue. She lived with her married sister for a while. On the strength of the resemblance alone I'd be willing to gamble that Minerva's father may have slept in more than one bed. The resemblance between Dorrie and Minerva is too striking to be coincidental.''

''You think Dorrie Ambler was kidnaped?'' Drake asked.

"I keep trying to convince myself she wasn't," Mason said. "And so far I haven't made much headway."

"I'm thinking about the time element," Drake said. "They'd have had a deuce of a time getting her out of the apartment house and down the stairs. They couldn't have used the elevator because that would have brought them back into our line of vision, or rather where we might have seen them. They couldn't afford to take that chance."

"I've been thinking about that, too," Mason said. "I'm wondering if perhaps they didn't keep her right there in the building."

"You mean they had another apartment?" Drake asked.

Mason nodded, thought for a moment, then said, "Check that phase of it, Paul. Try and find who has the apartments rented on the floor below and the floor above. There's just a chance they spirited her into another apartment."

"How about the shadowing jobs?"

"Call them off," Mason said. "The cops wouldn't like it, and shadows can't

159

do any good now.''

''Okay, Perry, I'll take a crack at that angle of another apartment.''

''And now,'' Della Street said, ''let's hope we can get the office routine back to some semblance of order, Mr. Perry Mason. You have a lot of canceled appointments and quite probably some irate clients.''

''And,'' Mason said, ''I know I have a stack of important mail that's unanswered and I suppose you're going to bring that up.''

''It will be on your desk within five minutes,'' she said.

Mason made a gesture of helplessness, turned to Paul Drake. ''Okay, Paul, back to the salt mines.''

Chapter Nine

As Perry Mason entered the office the next morning, Della Street said, "Good morning, Chief. I presume you've seen the papers."

"Actually I haven't," Mason said.

"Well, *you* certainly made the front page."

"The Ambler case?" Mason asked.

"According to the newspapers it's the Minden case. You can't expect a newspaper to waste headlines on an unknown when there's a voluptuous young heiress in the picture."

"And she's in the picture?" Mason asked.

"Oh, definitely. Cheesecake and all."

"She considered the occasion one for cheesecake?" Mason asked.

"Probably not, but the newspapers have a file on her, and she's posed for lots of cheesecake pictures. She has pretty legs — or hadn't you noticed?"

"I'd noticed," Mason confessed, picking up the newspaper which Della Street handed him, and standing at the corner of his desk, glancing at the headlines. He made a step toward his swivel chair, then remained standing, fascinated by what he was reading.

The telephone rang.

Della Street said, "Yes, Gertie." Then, "Just a minute. I'm sure he'll want to talk."

"Lieutenant Tragg," she said.

Mason put down the paper, moved over and picked up the telephone. "Hello, Lieutenant," Mason said. "I guess that your office was not only bugged but the bug must have been connected to one of the broadcasting studios."

"That's what I wanted to talk with you about," Tragg said. "I had to make a report, and the news got out from the report, not from me."

"You mean the release came from your superiors?"

"I'm not in a position to amplify that statement," Tragg said. "I'll say that the publicity came from the report and not from me."

"I see," Mason said.

"That is," Tragg amended, "the initial publicity. But after it appeared that the papers had the story, your client filled in the details."

"My client?" Mason asked.

"Minerva Minden."

"I've tried to tell you she's *not* my client. My client is Dorrie Ambler, who was abducted from the Parkhurst Apartments. . . . What have you found out about her, Lieutenant?"

"Precisely nothing, as far as I'm concerned," Tragg said. "I understand informally that the FBI is working on the case, although they haven't entered it officially as yet. You know how they are. Their purpose in life is to collect information, not to give it out."

"That would seem to be a logical attitude," Mason said. "I'm a little surprised at Minerva Minden. I thought perhaps she would prefer to have the story kept under wraps, but it's all here in the paper, all the details and ramifications, including the fact that this may reopen the entire question of her inheritance.''

''You'd think she wouldn't want that broadcast,'' Tragg said, ''but she's not particularly averse to newspaper notoriety.''

''I've noticed,'' Mason said.

''Well, I just wanted to call you up and explain.''

''Thanks for calling,'' Mason told him. ''I'm tremendously concerned about Dorrie Ambler.''

''I think you have a right to be,'' Tragg told him. ''We're doing everything we can, I know that. No matter whether it's an abduction or a murder and flight, we want to find her.''

''Will you let me know as soon as anything turns up?'' Mason asked.

Tragg's voice was cautious. ''Well, I'll either let you know or see that *she* has an opportunity to do so.''

"Thanks," Mason said. "And thanks again for calling."

"Okay," Tragg told him. "I just wanted you to know."

The lawyer cradled the telephone, returned to the newspaper.

"Well," he said at length, "it's certainly all in here — not only what she told them but some pretty shrewd surmises."

"What effect will that have," Della asked, "on the matter Dorrie Ambler wanted to have you work on?"

"She wanted to be sure she wasn't a Patsy," Mason said. "She wanted to have it appear that . . ."

"Yes?" Della Street prompted, as the lawyer suddenly stopped midsentence.

"You know," Mason said, "I keep trying to tell myself that it needn't have been an abduction — that this thing could have all been planned."

"Including the murder?"

"Not including the murder," Mason said. "We don't know what caused that murder, but we have a premise to start with. Our client was rather an intelligent young woman, and rather daring. She was quite willing to resort to unconventional methods in order to get one thing.''

''And that one thing?'' Della Street asked.

''Newspaper publicity,'' Mason said. ''She wanted to have the story of the look-alikes blazoned in the press. She *said* she wanted it because she didn't want to be set up as a Patsy in some crime she hadn't committed.''

Della Street nodded.

''Now of course,'' Mason said, ''that *may* not have been the real reason. The real reason may have been that she wanted to publicize her resemblance to Minerva Minden and then let the newspaper reporters get the bright idea they were related and have her case all built up in the newspapers.''

''And that would have helped her case in court?'' Della asked.

''Not only would it have been of help to her case in court,'' Mason said, ''but it would put her in a prime position to make a compromise with

Minerva Minden.''

Della Street nodded.

''But,'' Mason said, ''thanks to the quick thinking on the part of Minerva Minden, the scheme for newspaper publicity in connection with the airport episode fizzled out. So, under those circumstances, what would an alert young woman do?

''Try to think of some other scheme for getting her name in the papers,'' Della Street said.

Mason tapped the paper on the desk with the back of his hand.

''Well, I'll be darned,'' Della Street said. ''You think she arranged the whole business? The abduction, the —''

''There are certainly some things that indicate it,'' Mason said. ''I keep hoping that's the solution. It would have been difficult if not impossible for a man or two men to have taken an unwilling woman out of that apartment house. The police were on the scene within a matter of minutes. The way the elevator was placed they didn't dare use the elevator. They would have had to use the stairs.

Unless they had another apartment, they could hardly have taken her from the building."

Della's eyes were sympathetic. "You keep trying to convince yourself it was all part of a scheme," she said, "and I find myself trying to help you — even when I don't believe it."

Mason said, "It's quite a problem getting a woman to leave the house against her will."

"They could have held a gun on her, or a knife at her back," Della Street said.

"They could have," Mason said, "but remember that just about the time they reached the street the police cars were converging on the place."

"Would they have noticed her at that stage of the game?" Della Street asked.

"You're darned right they would," Mason said. "They are trained in that sort of thing. You'd be astounded to see what these officers can pick out of thin air. They've trained themselves to be alert. They have a sixth sense. They notice anything that is just a little bit out of the ordinary. At times it seems they're telepathic.

"If three people were walking down the sidewalk or into the parking lot — two men with an unwilling woman in between them — they'd have noticed it."

"You think there were two men?"

"I think the mattresses were dragged from the bedroom into the kitchen after Paul Drake and I rang the doorbell," Mason said. "I don't think one person would have had time to take two trips. I think there were two mattresses and therefore two persons dragging mattresses.

"Moreover, the problem of getting the girl out of the apartment house would have been almost insurmountable for one person. Remember that he had not only to get her out of the apartment house but he had to get her into a car and make a getaway. I keep thinking things will work out all right, that Dorrie knew what she was doing and that it was all part of a plan — all except the murder. The murder fouled things all up. That forced a change in plans — but Dorrie's all right — somewhere.''

Knuckles tapped a code signal on the door of the private office and at Mason's nod Della Street opened the door to let Paul Drake in.

''What's new, Paul?'' Mason asked.

''Quite a write-up in the papers,'' Drake said.

''Wasn't it?''

''The only thing it lacked was to have your picture alongside the cheesecake. The photograph they used of you was very somber and dignified.''

''They pulled it out of the newspaper's morgue,'' Mason said. ''They had to use what was available . . . . What's new, Paul?''

Drake said, ''It's possible, Perry, that your hunch about the apartment in the building could be an explanation.''

Mason's face etched into hard lines. ''How come, Paul?''

''The day before the abduction a man who gave his name as William Camas inquired about vacancies. He was told there was one on the eighth floor,

Apartment 805. He looked at it and said he wanted his wife to look at it, that he thought it would be all right. He put up a hundred dollars for what he termed an option for three days, with the understanding that at the end of three days he'd either sign a lease or forfeit the hundred dollars."

"And moved in?" Mason asked.

"Well, nobody knows for certain. The manager gave him the key to the apartment."

"And what's the condition of the apartment now? What does it indicate?" Mason asked. "Any fingerprints? Any —"

"Don't be silly," Drake said. "You thought of it and the police thought of it. The police started asking questions, found out about Camas and got a passkey to the apartment — and that's all anyone knows. The street comes to a dead end at that point. If the police found out anything, they're not passing out the information."

"But they did check the apartment?

"With a fine-toothed comb,"

Drake said.

"And do you know if they talked with Camas?"

"No one knows if they talked with Camas."

"You couldn't find him?"

"Not a trace," Drake said. "He gave a Seattle address. I've got my man checking it. My best guess is the address is phony."

The telephone rang. Della Street picked up the receiver, said, "Hello," then motioned to Drake. "For you, Paul."

Drake picked up the telephone, said, "Drake speaking," listened for a few minutes, said, "You're sure? . . . Okay, keep digging."

Drake hung up, turned to Perry Mason and said, "That's right. The address was a phony."

Mason said, "Hang it, Paul, that scuttles my last hope. I was banking on the theory they couldn't have got her out of that apartment against her will."

"I know," Drake said sympathetically. "I know how you feel,

but facts are facts. I have to give you the facts. That's my job.''

"Damn it,'' Mason said, ''we've got to *do* something, Paul. Wherever she is, she's counting on us for help.''

"Take it easy, Perry. A whole army of law enforcement people are working on the case. There's nothing more we could do except get in their way.''

"You're sure they're working on it?''

"Hell, yes, My man in Seattle found the Camas address was a phony. He was third in line. The Seattle police had been working on it, the Seattle FBI had been working on it.''

Mason said, ''That girl is in danger.''

"Not now she isn't,'' Drake said. ''I don't want to be heartless about it, but if anything's going to happen to her it's happened already. If she's dead, she's dead. If she isn't dead, it's because she's being held for some particular purpose, ransom or blackmail or something of that sort. There's just nothing you can do, Perry, except wait it out.''

Mason sighed. ''I have always been

accustomed to controlling events, within reason. I hate like hell to find myself in a position where events are controlling me."

"Well, they are now," Drake said. "There's nothing we can do except wait. I'm going back to the office, Perry, and I'll keep in touch."

"What about your men?" Mason asked. "Would it help to put more men out?"

"I'm calling them in," Drake said. "My men would simply run up an excessive bill for you to pay and they would get in the way of the law enforcement agencies that are working on the case. Let's just give them a free hand."

Mason was silent for several seconds, then said, "Okay, Paul."

Drake glanced at Della Street, then left the office.

Mason started dictating.

Halfway through the second letter the lawyer gave up, started pacing the office. "I can't do it, Della. I can't get my mind off — See if you can get

Lieutenant Tragg on the phone.''

She nodded sympathetically, went to the telephone and a few moments later nodded to Mason. "He's on the line, Chief."

Mason said, "Hello, Lieutenant. Perry Mason talking, and I'm worried about what's happening in the case of Dorrie Ambler. I'm just not satisfied with the way things are going."

"Who is?" Tragg countered.

"Have you found out anything?"

"We've found out a lot," Tragg said, "and we're trying to evaluate it, Perry."

"Can you tell me what it is?"

"Not all of it, no."

"What about this Apartment 805?"

"What do you know about that?"

"I'm asking you what you know."

"And I'm not in a position to tell you everything I know . . . . Look here, Perry. You aren't trying to slip a fast one over on us, are you?"

"What do you mean by that?"

"This isn't some elaborate scheme that you've thought up to serve as a smoke screen?"

"A smoke screen for what?" Mason asked.

"That's what I'd like to know," Tragg said.

"You're barking up the wrong tree, running off on a false scent, chasing a red herring and — Well, damn it, that's what I was afraid of, that you'd think this was some scheme or other I'd hatched up and would go at the whole business halfheartedly. I tell you, that girl is in danger."

"You're worried over the fact you didn't protect her from that danger? Tragg asked."

"Yes."

"All right, I can help you put your mind at rest on that point," Tragg said. "Your client wasn't a victim but an accomplice. She went from Apartment 907 down the stairs to Apartment 805. She remained there until after the heat was off. Then she left there willingly and under her own power."

"What gives you that idea?"

"An eyewitness."

Mason was silent for some seconds.

"Well?" Tragg asked.

Mason said, "Frankly, Lieutenant, you've relieved me a lot."

"In what way?"

"I have been aware of the possibility that this might be some part of an elaborate scheme."

"Not one that you thought up?"

"No, one that was intended to fool me as well as the police."

"Well, frankly, Perry, that's a theory that is being given more and more consideration by the investigators. And of course that leaves us with an unexplained murder on our hands. As you are probably aware, we don't like unexplained murders.

"Now, there's a very good possibility this whole deal was hatched up simply in order to account for the presence of a corpse in the apartment of your client. If it should turn out that's the case, we wouldn't like it."

"And I wouldn't like it," Mason said.

"All right," Tragg told him. "I'll put it right up to you, Perry. Is there some reason for you to believe — any good, legitimate reason — that your client may have been laying the foundation for a play of this sort?''

Mason said, ''I'll be fair with you, Tragg. There is just enough reason so that I have given the subject some consideration.

''If that girl has been abducted and is in danger, I can't just sit back and wait. If, on the other hand, this is part of an elaborate scheme to account for a murder, I'm not only going to wash my hands of her but I'd do anything I could to help solve the case and find out exactly what did happen. Of course I'd have to protect the confidence of my client because she was my client for a while.''

''I understand,'' Tragg said, ''but she wasn't your client as far as any murder case was concerned.''

''That's right. She wasn't — and I'll tell you something else. She isn't going to be.''

''Well,'' Tragg said, ''I'll tell you this much. I think you can wash your hands of the case. When she left that

178

apartment, she simply went downstairs and into Apartment 805. We know that later on that evening a woman who has an apartment on the sixth floor saw your client riding down in the elevator. The woman noticed her because despite the fact it was night Dorrie was wearing dark glasses and didn't want to be recognized. This woman had the idea Dorrie was going to some surreptitious trysting place and — My own private opinion, Mason, is that the witness may be just a little frustrated and a little envious.

"Anyway, she saw Miss Ambler in the elevator. She knows Dorrie Ambler and has chatted with her. Dorrie was fond of this woman's dog, and the dog was fond of Dorrie. It's a strange dog. He isn't vicious but he wants to be left alone. He growls if people move to pet him.

"Now, this woman witness saw that Dorrie Ambler for some reason didn't want to be recognized. Dorrie moved to the front of the elevator and kept her back to the woman and the dog, but the dog wanted her to pet him; he nuzzled her leg and wagged his tail. Well, after a minute Dorrie put her hand down and the dog licked her fingers. Then the elevator came to a stop and Dorrie hurried out."

"The woman was walking her dog, and the dog stopped when they got to the strip of lawn just outside the door, but the woman saw a man waiting in a car at the curb and Dorrie almost ran to the car, jumped in and was whisked away."

"Fingerprints?" Mason asked.

"None," Tragg said. "That's a strange thing. Both Apartments 907 and 805 have evidently been scrubbed clean as a whistle. There isn't a print in them except the prints of Marvin Billings. He left his prints all over Apartment 907."

"Did he have keys?" Mason asked.

"I shouldn't tell you this," Tragg said, "but I know how you feel.. There wasn't a single thing in Billings' pockets. No keys, no coins, no cigarettes, no pencil, nothing. He'd been stripped clean as a whistle."

Mason smiled. "Well, Lieutenant," he said, "you make me feel a lot better, even if it looks as if I have been victimized. You've lifted a great big load off my shoulders."

"All right, Perry," Tragg said. "I just want to warn you of one thing, that if this is a scheme that *you're* in on, you're going to get hurt. We don't like to have citizens arrange synthetic abductions and we don't like murder. And I can probably tell you without violating any confidence that Hamilton Burger, our district attorney, is firmly convinced that this is a hocus-pocus that has been thought up by you to confuse the issues so that when your client is finally apprehended he'll have a hard time convicting her of murder — and knowing Hamilton Burger as we both do, we know that this has made him all the more determined to expose the scheme and convict the plotters — *all* of them."

"I can readily understand that," Mason said. "Thanks for the tip, Lieutenant. I'll keep my nose clean."

"And your eyes open," Tragg warned.

"I will for a fact," Mason said as he hung up.

The lawyer turned to Della Street. "Well, Della, I guess we can get on with the mail now. I guess our erstwhile client was a pretty clever little girl and quite a schemer . . . . You listened in on Tragg's conversation?"

Della Street nodded, said suddenly and savagely, "I hope they catch her and convict her."

Then after a moment she added, "But if Dorrie Ambler had only played it straight and let you present her claim to the estate, she could have shared in several million dollars. Now she's got herself into a murder case."

Mason said, "That's something I don't have to worry about. After she's arrested, she can get a copybook, sit down and write 'honesty is the best policy' five hundred times."

"It'll be too late then," Della Street pointed out.

Mason arose and started pacing the

floor. "If it weren't for two things," he said at length, "I'd question the accuracy of Tragg's conclusions."

Della Street, knowing the lawyer wanted an excuse to think out loud, said, "What things, Chief?"

"First," Mason said, "we know that our client has been scheming up bizarre situations to attract publicity. We *know* she wanted to do something to make the newspapers publicize the resemblance between her and Minerva Minden."

"And the second thing?" Della asked.

"The dog," Mason said. "Dogs don't make mistakes. Therefore our client was alive, well, and navigating under her own power long after the supposed abduction.

"I guess, Della, we're going to have to accept the fact that Miss Dorrie Ambler decided to use me as a pawn in one of her elaborate schemes and then something happened that knocked her little schemes into a cocked hat."

"What?" Della asked.

"Murder," Mason said. "Billings was a detective with an unsavory reputation. Those on the inside who knew the game, knew he'd blackmail a client if the opportunity presented itself.''

''And so?'' Della asked.

''So,'' Mason said, ''realizing now Dorrie was merely trying to inveigle me into her scheme, knowing that she overreached herself, that she was perfectly free to call me long after her supposed abduction and didn't do so, I can wash my hands of her. I'm certainly glad you didn't walk into the trap of accepting that retainer, Della. As matters now stand, we did one piece of work for her and owe her nothing . . . . Now, thanks to a little dog, I can quit worrying. Let's get back to that pile of mail.''

Chapter Ten

Della Street, entering from the outer office, paused in front of Perry Mason's desk. When the lawyer looked up she said, "I hate to do this to you, Chief."

"What?" Mason asked.

"It's been ten days since Dorrie Ambler disappeared," Della Street said, "and you've managed to forget about it and get yourself back to a working schedule."

"Well?" Mason asked.

"Now," she said, "Henrietta Hull is in the outer office, waiting — impatiently."

"What does she want to see me about?"

"The police have picked up Minerva Minden. Henrietta Hull says she's not certain of the charges against her but she was told they were going to question her in connection with that murder."

Mason shook his head. "I'm representing Dorrie . . ."

Della Street raised inquiring eyebrows as Mason's voice trailed off into silence.

For some ten or fifteen seconds the lawyer was silent, then abruptly he said, "Bring her in, Della. I want to talk with her."

Della Street nodded, left the office and a few moments later returned with Henrietta Hull striding along in her wake.

"Mrs. Hull," Della Street announced.

"We've met," Henrietta Hull said, marching across to Mason's desk, giving him a firm grip with a bony hand, then seating herself in the client's chair.

"I told you, Mr. Mason, that you were at the top of our list on felony cases."

"And?" Mason asked, prompting her as she hesitated.

"Minerva has been taken into custody."

"Arrested?"

"I don't think so. They picked her up at three o'clock this morning to take her in for questioning. She hasn't returned and she hasn't telephoned."

"What do you want me to do?"

"Accept a retainer of twenty thousand dollars, go ahead and represent her."

"She is being questioned in connection with the murder of that man who was found in Apartment 907 — Marvin Billings?"

"I don't know. All I know is that they told her they wanted her to answer some questions in connection with a murder, that it was quite important."

"She rebelled at going with them at that hour in the morning?"

Henrietta Hull said, "As a matter of fact, she didn't. They evidently had been waiting for her. She was just getting in."

"Unescorted?" Mason asked.

"Unescorted."

"You were up at the time?"

"No. She left me a note explaining things. They let her do that. She said she would telephone. If I didn't hear from her by nine o'clock this morning, I was to go to you and give you a check for twenty thousand dollars as a retainer."

"You can write checks on her account?"

"Certainly. I'm her manager."

Henrietta Hull calmly opened her purse, took out a tinted oblong of paper, glanced at Della Street and said, "I presume your secretary takes the fees."

"That's the check?" Mason asked.

"Twenty thousand dollars," she said.

"I have tried to explain to you," Mason said, "that I have represented Dorrie Ambler and I'm afraid there is going to be a conflict of interest."

"You were only retained by Dorrie Ambler to keep her from being a Patsy, a fall guy, to use what is, I believe, the proper slang," Henrietta Hull said. "You gave her the advice she wanted and she left your office.

"For your information, Mr. Mason, Dorrie Ambler is a fraud and a cheat. She lied to you all the way through. You don't owe her anything. The young woman was an opportunist blackmailer. You definitely do not want to be tied up with her.''

Abruptly Paul Drake's code knock sounded on the door of the private office.

Mason said, ''Excuse me a moment,'' crossed the office, opened the door a crack and said, ''I'm busy, Paul. Can it wait?''

Drake said, ''It *can't* wait.''

Mason hesitated a moment.

''Come in,'' he said. ''You've met Mrs. Hull.''

Drake entered the office, said, ''Oh . . . hello. I don't want to interrupt, Mrs. Hull. However, it's necessary that I give Mr. Mason some information — at once.''

Henrietta Hull said, ''How do you do, Mr. Drake. I was going to drop in to see you as soon as I had finished with Mr. Mason, or perhaps I should say, as soon as he had finished with me. I explained to you that I keep a list of people to whom I should turn in the event of

189

serious trouble.

"Mr. Mason heads the list of attorneys in connection with felony cases, and your agency heads the list as an investigating agency, particularly in cases where Mr. Mason acts as counsel.

"I have just given Mr. Mason a check as a retainer and I have here in my purse a check made out to you for twenty-five hundred dollars as retainer."

"Now, just a minute," Mason interrupted. "Miss Minden was picked up this morning for questioning. That's about all you know about it. It was questioning in connection with a murder. She hasn't communicated with you and apparently you haven't communicated with the police or the prosecutor in order to find out what has happened, yet you have made out checks totaling twenty-two thousand, five hundred dollars and are seeking to retain counsel for her and a detective agency to investigate facts."

"That's right."

"You say that you are following instructions given to you in a note by Miss Minden?"

"Yes."

"Do you have that note with you?"

"Actually I have."

"I think I'd like to see it," Mason said.

She hesitated a moment, then said, "Can I be assured that the contents will be confidential if I show it to you, Mr. Mason?"

Mason shook his head.

Drake said, "I want to talk with you alone, Perry."

"About this case?" Mason asked.

"Yes."

"I think you'd better talk right here," Mason said. "I think we'd better have this out in a joint session, so to speak."

"All right," Drake said. "Dorrie Ambler is dead. She was murdered. Her body has been uncovered, and police have what they consider an airtight case against Minerva Minden."

Mason pushed back his chair, got to his feet, stood in frowning concentration for a moment, then walked around the corner of his desk over to the window, turned his back to the interior of the office, looked down at the street for a few minutes, turned around, said to Henrietta Hull, "If what Paul Drake says is true, Mrs. Hull, your employer is in a most serious predicament; exceedingly serious."

"I understand that."

"Did you know Miss Ambler was dead?"

"I knew the police said . . . that they had discovered her body — yes."

"Let me ask you this: Is Minerva guilty?"

"She is *not* guilty," Henrietta Hull said with firm conviction.

"How do you know she isn't guilty? Simply because of what you know of her?"

"No. Because of what I know of the case. Dorrie teamed up with a couple of crooks. They killed her. Now they want to blame that murder on Minerva. Miss Ambler tried to pull a fast one. Her scheme boomeranged. Minerva is not guilty of anything. Does all this make a difference about your taking Minerva's case?"

"It makes a difference," Mason said. "Technically no matter how guilty a person may be he is not convicted until final judgment has been passed. He is entitled to have an attorney at every stage of the proceedings; not necessarily in order to prove him innocent but to see that all his legal rights are protected."

"And Minerva would have that right as a citizen?"

"She would have that right as a citizen."

"She wants you as her attorney."

Drake cleared his throat, caught Mason's eye, imperceptibly shook his head.

"Why not, Paul? Come out with it," Mason said. "Let not be beating around the bush or equivocating."

"All right," Drake said. "Police have got an airtight case against her."

"You said that before."

"Her accomplice has confessed," Drake said.

"Who was it?" Mason asked.

"The man she hired to accompany her to Dorrie Ambler's apartment

193

and abduct her.''

''He says Minerva was with him at that time?'' Mason asked.

''I understand that he does.''

''Do you know the details, Paul?''

''Only generalities. This fellow's name is Jasper. He says that Minerva told him that she had inherited a fortune, that Dorrie Ambler stood in the way of her keeping exclusive control of the estate, that she wanted Dorrie Ambler out of the way, that she would arrange a background which would give them absolute protection but she wanted Jasper to help her at the proper time.

''Jasper, incidentally, has a long criminal record. Billings tried to blackmail Minerva, not Dorrie Ambler. He wound up with a fatal bullet in his chest.''

''And they've arrested Minerva Minden for the murder of Dorrie Ambler?''

Drake shook his head. ''They're going to prosecute her for the murder of Marvin Billings. Then, in case she should get an acquittal or a verdict that didn't carry the death penalty, they're going to prosecute her for the murder of Dorrie Ambler. The Ambler murder depends on circumstantial evidence. They've got the deadwood evidence, several admissions and an eyewitness in the Marvin Billings murder. Minerva can never beat *that* rap.

Mason reached a sudden decision. He said, "I'll represent her on the murder of Marvin Billings. If that's the murder she's being charged with, I'll be her attorney in that case. I won't promise to represent her if she is being charged with the murder of Dorrie Ambler. I'd have to think that one over."

"Fair enough," Henrietta Hull said. "Consider yourself retained, Mr. Mason."

"Just a minute," Mason said. "If you haven't communicated with her, how do you know that the case on which she's being prosecuted is the Billings murder and not the Dorrie Ambler murder?"

Henrietta Hull hesitated for just the bat of an eyelash, then said, "Frankly, I don't, Mr. Mason. But if it should turn out to be the other way around, you could always give back the retainer and withdraw from the case. It would be all right with us.''

Mason said, ''Let me take a look at that note that Minerva left for you.''

Henrietta Hull opened her purse, took out a folded piece of paper and handed it to Mason.

The note read: ''Henny — Going to Headquarters. If I'm not in by nine do the necessary.''

''There are no specific instructions in this letter,'' Mason said. ''Certainly none to retain me or to call on the Drake Detective Agency.''

''I think you're mistaken, Mr. Mason. She said, and I quote, *'Do the necessary.'* ''

''Does that mean that you and Minerva had discussed this matter in advance?''

''It means,'' she said, ''that Minerva trusted my discretion to do the necessary and I am doing it.''

''Now look,'' Drake said, ''I'm not going to hang any crepe, but there have been two deliberate cold-blooded murders here. One of them was carefully planned in advance. The other *may* have been done in the heat of passion. But they've now got an open-and-shut case against Minerva Minden. You know it and I know it. They have eyewitnesses. They wouldn't have dared touch her with a ten-foot pole if they didn't have the deadwood.''

Mason, who had been frowning thoughtfully, said, ''Give Mrs. Hull a receipt for twenty thousand dollars as a retainer fee, Della.''

Chapter Eleven

Perry Mason, seated in the consulting room in the jail building, looked across at Minerva Minden and said, "Minerva, before you say a word to me, I want to tell you that Henrietta Hull called on me this morning. She gave me a check for twenty thousand dollars as a retainer to represent you. I told her that I would defend you on the charge of murdering Marvin Billings; that I couldn't as yet tell whether I would defend you on the charge of murdering Dorrie Ambler."

"As I understand it," she said, "the Billings murder is the one on which I am being held."

"Has a formal complaint been signed?"

"I believe they're intending to have

an indictment by the grand jury and for some reason they want to have the trial itself take place just as soon as possible — and that suits me.''

''Ordinarily,'' Mason said, ''we spar for time in a criminal case and try to see what develops.''

''This isn't an ordinary case,'' she said.

''I'm satisfied it isn't,'' Mason told her. ''I'm beginning to have a glimmering of what *I* think happened.''

She took her head and said, ''I don't think you know enough of the facts to reach any conclusion.''

''Perhaps I don't,'' Mason said. ''I am going to ask you one question. Did you murder Marvin Billings?''

''No.''

''At the moment that's all I want to know,'' Mason said.

''All right,'' she told him. ''Now I have a confession to make to you. I —''

''Is this to confess a crime?'' Mason interposed.

''Yes, but it's —''

Mason held up his hand. ''I don't

want to hear *any* confession.''

''This isn't what you think it is. It doesn't relate to —''

''How do *you* know what *I'm* thinking?'' Mason interrupted.

She said, ''Because this is something that would never have occurred to you. It's about another matter entirely. It doesn't have to do with this murder, it has to do with —''

Mason said, ''Hold it, Minerva. I want to explain my position to you. You've told me that you're innocent of the murder on which you're going to be tried. If you have lied to me, that is your hard luck, because it's going to put me in a position where I'll be acting on a false assumption.

''Now then, any confession which you may want to make is entirely different.

''Any communication made by a client to an attorney is a privileged communication, but if you tell me that you have committed some particular crime, particularly if it's a different crime from the one you're charged with, the situation becomes different. I am

200

your attorney but I am also a citizen. I can advise you in connection with your legal rights, but if I know that you have committed a serious crime and then try to advise you what to do to avoid being apprehended for that crime, I put myself in the position of being an accessory.

"I don't want to get put in that positon."

She thought that over for a few seconds, then said, "I see."

"Now," Mason went on, "you must realize that they have a lot against you — some perfectly devastating evidence that clinches the case in their minds. Otherwise they would never have dared to proceed in this manner. They would have gone to your home and very courteously asked you questions. Then they would have checked on your answers, asked you more questions and eventually would have instituted proceedings only after they had convinced themselves of your guilt.

"The manner in which they're acting at the present time indicates that they have some deadly bit of evidence which they are counting on to bring about a conviction, and which probably is going to take you by surprise — or at least they think it's going to take you by surprise."

"From their questions," she said, "I gathered that this man, Dunleavey Jasper, had told them quite a story."

"Involving you?"

"Yes."

"What dealings have you had with Dunleavey Jasper?"

"None."

"Have you ever seen him?"

"I think I have."

"When?"

"Two detectives brought a man into the office when I was being interrogated by the prosecutor. The man looked at me, looked at the prosecutor, nodded, and then they took him out."

Mason thought that over for a few seconds, suddenly got up, said, "All right, Miss Minden, I'm going to represent you. But I just want to point out that some of the things you have been doing are not going to be conducive to securing acquittal.

"You've more or less deliberately played up to the press in their characterization of you as the madcap heiress of Montrose.

"In addition to the things which you have done, and which have been documented, there's a lot of whispering about nude swimming parties and things of that sort."

"All right," she said, "what of it? It's my body, I like it and it's beautiful. I'm not dumb enough to think that it isn't.

"People go to nudist camps and everybody takes those camps for granted and leaves nudists alone, but if a person is reasonably broadminded and objects to the —"

"You don't need to argue with *me*," Mason said, smiling, "but I'm simply telling you that many a person has violated the moral code and then been unfortunate enough to be charged with murder. Jurors of a certain type love to throw the book at someone who has violated their particular moral code.

"Many an unfortunate individual has been convicted of murder on evidence that proved he or she was guilty of adultery."

"All right," she said, "in the eyes of many people I'm a scarlet woman. Is that going to keep you from taking my case?"

"No."

"Is it going to interfere with my chances of an acquittal?"

"Yes."

"Thanks, Mr. Mason," she said. "I wondered if you'd be frank or whether you'd engage in a lot of double talk. You don't need to tell me anything about the hatchet-faced frustrated biddies who love to sit in judgment on their fellow women."

"What I was trying to point out," Mason said, "was that when a young woman tries to emancipate herself from the conventions and goes out of her way to build up a reputation for being a madcap heiress, it sometimes proves embarrassing."

"If she gets charged with murder,"

Minerva said.

"And you're charged with murder," Mason pointed out.

"Thank you for the lecture," she said. "I'll try and be a good girl after I get out. At least I'll keep my name out of the papers."

Mason said, "Apparently you have no realization of what's going to happen. You're good copy. The fact that you're charged with murder is going to sell papers, and when something happens that sells papers it gets played up big."

"I take it you mean really big," she said.

"I mean really big," Mason told her. "That brings up the picture I want to present to the public — a rather demure but highly active young women who is bighearted, acts on impulse, and is sometimes misunderstood; but at heart you're rather demure."

"That's the face you want me to present to the public?"

"Yes."

"To hell with it," she said, shaking her head. "I'm not going to try to change my personality just to beat a murder rap. That's up to you, Mr. Perry Mason. I'm not demure and I'm not going to put on that mask for public comsumption in the press.''

Mason sighed as he picked up his brief case and started for the door. "I was afraid you'd have that attitude," he said.

"I've got it," she told him. "And now you know."

Chapter Twelve

Judge Everson Flint glanced at the deputy district attorney who was seated with Hamilton Burger at the prosecutor's counsel table. "The peremptory is with the People."

"We pass the peremptory," the deputy announced.

Judge Flint looked at the defense table. "The peremptory is with the defense, Mr. Mason."

Mason stood up and made a geture of acceptance, a gesture which somehow managed to be as eloquent as a thousand words. "The defense," he said, "is *completely* satisfied with the jury."

"Very well," Judge Flint said, "the jury will be sworn."

The deputy district attorney sneeringly

mimicked Mason's gesture of moving the left hand outward. "There's no need to make a speech about it," he said.

Mason's smile in the direction of the prosecutor's table was deliberately irritating. "Why try then?"

Judge Flint said, "Let's try and get along without personalities, gentlemen. The jury will now be sworn to the case."

After the jury had been sworn, Colton Parma, the deputy, at a nod from Hamilton Burger, the district attorney, made the opening statement.

"This is going to be a very brief opening statement, if it please the Court, and you, ladies and gentlemen of the jury," he said. "We propose to show that the defendant in this case inherited a fortune from Harper Minden. But she had reason to believe that there were other relatives of Harper Minden who were entitled to share in the estate; specifically, a young woman named Dorrie Ambler, who was the daughter of the defendant's mother's sister.

"The sister had died unmarried and it

was presumed she had left no issue. However, we will introduce evidence showing that the defendant, by her own statement, had unearthed evidence that Dorrie Ambler was actually the daughter of her mother's sister, born out of wedlock, and that she and the defendant *had the same father*.

"We are not going to try to confuse the issues in the case by going into the intricacies of the law. We are simply setting forth the facts as I have explained them to you in order to show the state of mind of the defendant.

"The defendant was at the Montrose Country Club attending a dance on the night of September sixth. Liquor was served, and the defendant had had several drinks. She had an altercation with her escort, decided to leave him, and left the country club in a fit of anger.

"We expect to show that the defendant is spoiled, impulsive, and somewhat arrogant at times. She found an automobile in the parking place that had the keys in it and the motor running.

It was a Cadillac automobile with license number WHW 694 and it had been stolen from an owner in San Francisco, although the defendant had no means of knowing that at the time. The defendant jumped in this stolen car and drove away, apparently intending to go home.

"At the intersection of Western Avenue and Hollywood Boulevard she went through a stop signal, struck a pedestrian, hesitated a moment, jumped out of the car, started to go to the injured pedestrian, then changed her mind, jumped back in the car and drove rapidly away.

"Now, I wish to impress upon you, ladies and gentlemen of the jury, that any evidence which will be introduced tending to connect the defendant with hit-and-run, or with any other violation of the law, is introduced solely for the purpose of showing the background of the present case *and the motivation of the defendant*.

"We will show that the defendant concocted a brilliant scheme for absolving herself of liability. She hired a firm of private detectives and placed an ad in the newspaper offering employment to a young woman who had a certain particular physical description.

"She instructed the persons who were screening the applicants for that job to get someone who was as near a physical double as possible.

"Dorrie Ambler answered that ad. As soon as the person in charge of screening the applicants saw her, it was realized that Dorrie Ambler bore a startling resemblance to the defendant; a resemblance so striking that it aroused the defendant's suspicion that Dorrie Ambler must be related to her and in short must be the illegitimate daughter of her mother's sister.

"We propose to introduce evidence showing that the scheme hatched by the defendant was to have Dorrie Ambler walk by the witnesses who had seen the defendant at the time of the hit-and-run accident. She hoped that Dorrie Ambler would be identified by those witnesses.

"Once they had made a mistaken

identification, the defendant felt that *she* herself would be immune from subsequent prosecution.

"However, when she saw the manner in which Dorrie Ambler resembled her, the defendant realized that she had set in chain a sequence of events which she couldn't control. She knew that the newspapers would seize upon that resemblance and would soon find out that the two girls were actually closely related.

"It was at this point that the defendant entered into a conspiracy with one Dunleavey Jasper, who had tracked her down, and as a result of that conspiracy —"

"Now, just a minute," Mason said. "We dislike interrupting the prosecution's opening statement, but the prosecution is now bringing in evidence of other crimes with the purpose of prejudicing the jury. We assign the remarks as misconduct and ask the Court to admonish the prosecutor and at the same time to instruct the jury to ignore those remarks."

"We know exactly what we are doing," Parma said to Judge Flint. "We will stand on the record. We are entitled to introduce evidence of *any* crimes as motivation for the murder with which this defendant is being charged."

Judge Flint said to the jury, "It is the law that a defendant being tried for one crime cannot be presumed guilty because of evidence of other crimes, except where such evidence is for the purpose of showing motivation. In view of the assurance of the prosecutor that that is the case here, I warn you that you are not to pay any attention to any evidence of any other crimes alleged to have been committed by this defendant, or to any evidence indicating the commission of such crimes, except for the purpose of showing motivation for the murder of the decedent, Marvin Billings.

"Proceed, Mr. Deputy, and please be careful to limit your remarks."

"We know exactly what we are doing, Your Honor," Parma said. "Our remarks are limited and will be limited. The evidence of other crimes is solely

213

for the purpose of showing motivation.''

"Very well, proceed,'' Judge Flint said.

"I am virtually finished, Your Honor.'' Parma turned to the jury. "We expect to show that Dunleavey Jasper traced the stolen car to the possession of the defendant, that the defendant learned Dunleavey Jasper had a criminal record and that the car was stolen; that she thereupon conspired with Dunleavey Jasper to abduct Dorrie Ambler so that she could be removed as a possible applicant for a share of the Minden estate, and to discredit Miss Ambler by making it seem Dorrie Ambler had been the hit-and-run driver.

"We expect to show that in the course of carrying out this conspiracy the private detective, Marvin Billings, found out what was happening. I think it is a reasonable inference which you can draw from the evidence that Billings tried to blackmail the defendant.

"Had it not been that Marvin Billings felt that the remarkable resemblance between these women was due to a common ancestry, had he not felt he could work with Dorrie Ambler to get a share of the Harper Minden estate, this case would never have been brought to trial because then there would have been no murder.

"We hold no brief for the dead man. The evidence will show you he was in effect playing both ends against the middle. But no matter how cunning he may have been, no matter how low he may have been, the law protects him. His life was a human life. His killing was murder.

"So Marvin Billings went to the apartment of Dorrie Ambler, and his arrival was at the moment when Miss Ambler was being spirited down to another apartment on the floor below.

"Billings sounded the chimes. After a moment's hesitation, the defendant opened the door, trusting to her resemblance to Dorrie Ambler to carry off the scene.

"At first Billings was deceived, but when he kept talking to the defendant he soon realized the impersonation. That was when he tried blackmail, and that was when the defendant shot him with a twenty-two revolver.

"Shortly after the shooting of Billings, the chimes on the apartment door sounded again.

"We expect to show you that the persons then at the door were none other than Perry Mason, the attorney for the defense, and Paul Drake, a private detective.

"The conspirators had to get out of the back door of the apartment. Acting upon the assumption that their callers did not know of this back door, they hurriedly dragged mattresses from the twin beds in the bedroom across the living room into the kitchenette, and by using a kitchen table and the mattresses, barricaded the door.

"When Mason and Paul Drake entered the apartment which they did after a few minutes, they found Marvin Billings unconscious and in a dying condition. They found the kitchen door barricaded in such a way that they thought for a while it was being held against their efforts to open it by someone in the kitchen.

"We expect to show that the unfortunate Dorrie Ambler, having been taken to Apartment 805, was given a hypodermic injection of morphia against her will and —"

"Now, just a moment," Mason said. "Again we are going to interrupt the deputy district attorney and object to any evidence of what may have happened to Dorrie Ambler."

"It goes to show motive," Parma said.

"It can't show motive for the murder of Marvin Billings," Mason said, "because what the deputy prosecutor is talking about now is something that occurred after the shooting of Marvin Billings."

"I think that is right," Judge Flint ruled.

"Very well, if I am going to be limited in my proof . . . I'll pass this matter on my opening statement, ladies and gentlemen, but we expect to introduce proof and we will have a

217

ruling on the matter as the witnesses come on the stand.

"I am not going to weary you with details. I have told you the general nature of the case so you can understand the evidence you will hear. You will hear the confession of one of the members of this consiracy and you will hear evidence of admissions made by the defendant herself.

"We are going to ask a verdict of first-degree murder at your hands. However, as far as this trial is concerned, it is only necessary for you to determine just one thing."

Parma held up his left index finger high above his head. "Just one thing, ladies and gentlemen," he said, shaking the outstretched finger. "That is, whether or not the evidence in this case proves the defendant guilty of the crime of murder, the killing of Marvin Billings.

"We shall ask a verdict of guilty at your hands, a verdict of first-degree murder."

Parma turned and walked back to his

seat at the prosecutor's table.

"Do you wish to make an opening statement, Mr. Mason?"

"No," Mason said, "except that I wish the Court to admonish the jury that the statement of the prosecutor was inaccurate as a matter of law."

"In what respect?" Judge Flint asked.

Mason arose and extended his left hand above his head, extending the left forefinger. "It isn't a matter, Your Honor, of proving just one thing: whether the evidence shows the defendant guilty. It is a matter of proving two things."

And Mason slowly raised his right hand and extended the right index finger. "It is a question of proving the defendant guilty beyond all reasonable doubt. I think the Court should so advise the jury."

"Well, I think the jury understands that in any criminal case the evidence must prove the defendant guilty beyond all reasonable doubt."

"Otherwise the defendant is entitled to a verdict of acquittal."

"The Court will cover that matter in its instructions," Judge Flint said.

Mason slowly lowered his hands with the extended forefingers and seated himself.

Judge Flint repressed a smile at the skillful manner in which Perry Mason, waiving his opening statement, had nevertheless scored a telling point on the prosecution.

"Call your first witness," Judge Flint said to the prosecutor.

"I will call Emily Dickson."

Mrs. Dickson, a rather attractive woman in her early forties, took the oath and seated herself on the witness stand after giving her name and address.

"What was your occupation on the sixth of September?" Parma asked

"I was the manager of the Parkhurst Apartments."

"You were residing there in the apartments?"

"I was."

"Did you know Dorrie Aambler in her lifetime?"

"Just a minute," Mason said. "If the

Court please, I ask that the jury be admonished to disregard that question. I ask that the prosecutor be cited for misconduct. I object to any statement intimating that Dorrie Ambler is dead. It assumes a fact not in evidence.''

"I didn't say she was dead," Parma said. "I merely asked the witness if she knew Dorrie Ambler during her lifetime. That's a perfectly permissible question. I can always ask that about anybody. I could ask her if she knew you during your lifetime.''

"The inference is that the person inquired about is no longer alive," Mason said, "and I feel the question was deliberately slanted so as to convey that impression.''

"I think so too," Judge Flint said. "Now, gentlemen, let's not have any misunderstanding about this. I am willing to permit the prosecution to introduce evidence of any other crime, provided that evidence is necessarily pertinent to the present question before the jury, for the purpose of showing motive or method or a general pattern

221

within the provisions of the rule with which I am quite sure you are all familiar.

"I have ruled that there is not going to be any evidence introduced of any crime committed *after* the alleged crime in this case was completed."

"I'll withdraw the question," Parma said with poor grace.

Judge Flint said, "I advise the jury to disregard the question and any insinuation contained in the question or any thoughts which may have been placed in your minds because of the nature of the question. I am going to state further to the prosecutor that I will declare a mistrial in the event there are any further attempts to circumvent the ruling of the Court."

"I wasn't trying to circumvent the ruling of the Court," Parma said.

"Well," Judge Flint observed dryly, "you're too much of a veteran not to know the effect of your question. Now I suggest that you proceed, and be *very* careful."

"Very well," Parma said, turning to

the witness. "Did you know Dorrie Ambler prior to the sixth of September?"

"Yes."

"For how long had you known her prior to September sixth?"

"Approximately — oh, I guess five or six months."

"Miss Ambler had an apartment in Parkhust Apartments?"

"She did."

"Where was it?"

"Apartment 907."

"Now I'm going to ask you if you also rented Apartment 805 prior to the twelfth day of September, and if so, do you know the name of the tenant?"

"I do now. His name is Dunleavey Jasper, but at the time he told me he was William Camas."

"*When* did you rent him Apartment 805?"

"On the eleventh of September."

"Of this year?"

"Yes."

"I have some further questions to ask this witness upon another phase of the matter," Parma said, "but I will put the witness on the stand at a later date."

"Very well," Judge Flint said, turning to Mason. "Cross-examine."

"Can you describe Dorrie Ambler?" Mason asked.

"Yes. She was about twenty-five or six."

"Eyes?"

"Hazel."

"Hair?"

"Auburn."

"General appearance?"

"She was almost the exact image of the defendant in this case, the woman sitting there at your left."

"Oh, you notice the resemblance, do you?" Mason asked.

"I notice a very distinct resemblance — a startling resemblance."

"Did you ever comment on it?"

"I certainly did."

"Would it be possible to confuse the defendant with Dorrie Ambler and vice versa?"

"It would be very possible."

"When did you first see the

defendant?''

"When she was placed in a show-up box.''

"And at that time you identified her as Dorrie Ambler, didn't you?'' Mason asked.

"Objection,'' Parma said. "Incompetent, irrelevant and immaterial. Not proper cross-examination.''

"Overruled,'' Judge Flint snapped.

"Well, I had been told that I was going to be called on to pick out Minerva Minden and I told them —''

"Never mind what *you* told *them*,'' Mason said. "What did *they* tell *you*?''

"That they wanted me to pick out Minerva Minden.''

"And did you tell them you had never seen Minerva Minden before?''

"Yes.''

"But they still wanted you to identify a woman you had never seen?''

"They wanted me to see if she resembled Dorrie Ambler.''

"And you saw her in the show-up box?''

"Yes.''

"And noticed her resemblance?"

"Yes."

"How close a resemblance?"

"A very striking resemblance."

"I'm going to repeat," Mason said. "Did you identify the defendant as Dorrie Ambler?"

"Objection, Your Honor," Parma said.

"Overruled," Judge Flint snapped.

"Yes, I did. I told them that was Dorrie Ambler that they had in the show-up box and then they convinced me —"

"Never mind what they convinced you about," Mason said. "I'm just trying to find out what happened. Did you identify the woman in the show-up box as being Dorrie Ambler?"

"At first I did. Yes."

"Oh, you made two identifications?"

"Well, they told me that — Well, if I'm not allowed to say what they told me I — Well, first I identified her as Dorrie Ambler and then I identified her as Minerva Minden."

"Despite the fact you had never seen

Minerva Minden?''

"I had seen her picture."

"Where?"

"In the newspapers. That was how it happened that the police called on me in the first place."

"How did they know you had seen her picture in the papers?"

"I rang them up and told them that the picture in the paper of Minerva Minden was actually the picture of Dorrie Ambler who had rented the apartment from me."

"So then the police came to talk with you?"

"Yes."

"When did Dorrie Ambler rent the apartment from you?"

"In May."

"And how do you know it wasn't the defendant, Minerva Minden, who rented the apartment from you?"

"Because I didn't know her at that time. I had never seen her at that time."

"But you admitted that you couldn't tell her from Dorrie Ambler."

"Oh, but I could, Mr. Mason. After I

realized the resemblance and studied the defendant, as I told you, I made a second identification. I said after looking more closely, that the woman I had identified as Dorrie Ambler was someone who looked very much like her, but it wasn't Miss Ambler.''

"At that time you were certain Miss Minden, the defendant, was *not* the person who had rented the apartment?''

"Absolutely certain.''

"Because of things the police had told you?''

"No. There were other means, other reasons. I convinced myself.''

"Thank you,'' Mason said. "No further cross-examination.''

Parma said, "You may step down, Mrs. Dickson.

"Now then, I am going to call Lieutenant Tragg to the stand very briefly, simply for a matter of identification.''

"Very well, Lieutenant Tragg to the stand,'' Judge Flint ordered.

Tragg came forward, was sworn, testified that he had gone to Apartment

907 at the Parkhurst Apartments in response to a call, that he had found there a man in a dying condition; that the man was subsequently identified as Marvin Billings, a private detective.

"Now, what happened to Mr. Billings?"

"He died."

"When?"

"He died on the way to the Receiving Hospital. He was dead on arrival. He had been shot in the chest and that wound proved fatal. That was on the twelfth day of September."

"And how soon did he leave the apartment after you first saw him? That is, when did the ambulance take him away?"

"Within a matter of ten minutes — well, fifteen minutes at the outside."

"Thank you," Parma said. "You may cross-examine."

"No questions," Mason said.

"Call Delbert Compton," Parma said.

Compton, a competent-appearing, heavy-set individual in his early fifties, eased himself into position in the witness chair and surveyed the courtroom with steely, watchful eyes.

"Your name is Delbert Compton, you reside in this city and are now and for some years last past have been the junior partner and manager of the Billings & Compton Detective Agency?"

"Yes, sir."

"You handle most of the office work, and your partner, Marvin Billings, was in charge of the outside operations?"

"Yes, sir."

"If the Court please," Hamilton Burger said, getting to his feet, "I think my associate is a little hesitant about pointing out that this man is a hostile witness. I would like to have the Court rule that he is a hostile witness and give us permission to ask leading questions."

"He has shown no hostility so far," Judge Flint said. "When the matter reaches that point, in case it does reach that point, you may then renew your motion. For the present the Court will take it under advisement. Go ahead, Mr. Parma."

"Were you carrying on your business

in this city on the sixth of September?''

"Yes, sir."

"During the month of September were you employed by the defendant in this case?''

"Well . . . I suppose so . . . yes."

"Who employed you?"

"The defendant's representative, Henrietta Hull. I believe Mrs. Hull is her manager.''

"And what was the purpose of the employment?''

"I was instructed to put an ad in the paper, an ad asking for unattached women of a certain description."

"Did you put such an ad in the paper?''

"I did."

"The compensation was rather high?''

"A thousand dollars a month."

"Then what did you do?"

"I had one of my female operatives rent a suite in a hotel and interview applicants.''

"And what instructions did you give your female operative?''

"Objected to," Mason said, "as

incompetent, irrelevant and immaterial, hearsay, a conversation taking place outside of the hearing of the defendant.''

''Sustained,'' Judge Flint said.

''All right, I'll put it this way,'' Parma said. ''What instructions were you told by Henrietta Hull to give your operative?''

''She didn't tell me.''

''She didn't tell you what to do?'' Parma asked.

''I didn't say that. I said she didn't tell me what instuctions to give my operative.''

Parma looked at Judge Flint somewhat helplessly.

''All right,'' Judge Flint said, ''take your ruling. Ask leading questions.''

''I'll put it this way,'' Parma said. ''Didn't Henrietta Hull, acting on behalf of the defendant in this case, advise you in general terms to arrange an elaborate setup for interviewing applicants, but that their qualifications had nothing whatsoever to do with their ultimate selection, that you were to wait until a young woman came in who resembled a photograph which she gave you. That you were to hire the person who had the closest resemblance to that photo."

The witness hesitated for a long time.

"Answer the question," Judge Flint said.

"Well . . . yes."

"Didn't you hire a young woman named Dorrie Ambler, and didn't she telephone you each day at an unlisted number in order to get instructions as to what she was to do?"

"Yes."

"And didn't you report to Henrietta Hull that you had been able to hire not only an applicant who looked like the young woman in the photograph, but had hired the person shown in the photograph?"

"Yes."

"And didn't Henrietta Hull say that was impossible and didn't you tell her to see for herself, that you'd have this woman walk across a certain intersection at a fixed time and that Henrietta Hull could make surreptitious observations so as to convince herself?"

"Yes."

"And didn't Henrietta Hull then tell you to start looking up this young woman's background?"

"Yes."

"And didn't you, in pursuance of instructions given by Henrietta Hull, get this woman to walk back and forth, up and down Hollywood Boulevard in the vicinity of the Western Avenue intersection to see if a witness, Mrs. Ella Granby, wouldn't identify her as the person driving the car involved in a hit-and-run accident on September sixth?"

"Well, no, not exactly."

"What do you mean, not exactly?"

"I didn't tell her all that."

"But you did tell her to walk up and down Hollywood Boulevard near the intersection of Western?"

"Well . . . yes."

"And to report to you anything that happened?"

"Yes."

"And she did report that a woman had made an identification?"

"Yes."

"And didn't you then advise her that she could take the next day off and didn't need to do anything?"

"I can't remember my detailed instructions but something of that sort probably happened."

"And all of that was under instructions from Henrietta Hull?"

"Yes."

"You were reporting to Henrietta Hull regularly?"

"Yes."

"Cross-examaine," Parma snapped.

Mason said, "How did you know Henrietta Hull was the representative of the defendant?"

"She told me so."

"In a conversation?"

"Yes."

"In person or over the telephone?"

"Over the telephone."

"Then you have never seen Henrietta Hull. Is that correct?"

"That is correct. I talked with her over the telephone."

"You received compensation for your work?"

"Yes."

"Did you bill the defendant for that?"

"No, I did not."

"Why?"

"I was paid in advance."

"Who paid you?"

"I received the money from Henrietta Hull."

"In the form of a check?"

"In the form of cash."

"But if you have never met Henrietta Hull, she couldn't have given you the cash."

"She sent it to me."

"How?"

"By messenger."

"How much?"

"Thirty-five hundred dollars."

"Did you see Dorrie Ambler personally?"

"Yes."

"And you have seen the defendant?"

"More recently, yes. I am, of course, looking at her now."

"Was there a striking physical resemblance between Dorrie Ambler and the defendant?"

"A very striking resemblance."

Mason held his eyes on the witness. "For all you know, Mr. Compton," he said, "you were hired, not by the defendant, *but by Dorrie Ambler.*"

"*What?*" the witness asked, startled.

"Dorrie Ambler," Mason said, "wanted to establish a claim to the Harper Minden estate. She wanted a certain amount of notoriety in order to launch her campaign. She needed newspaper publicity. So she rang you up and told you she was Henrietta Hull and —"

"Just a minute, just a minute," Parma shouted, jumping to his feet. "All this assumes facts not in evidence. It consists of a statement by counsel and I object to it on —"

"I withdraw the question," Mason said, smiling, "and ask it this way. Mr. Compton, *if* Dorrie Ambler had wanted to attract attention to her remarkable similarity to the defendant in this case, and *if* she had called you up, told you she was Henrietta Hull and had asked you to put that ad in the paper and to hire Dorrie Ambler when she showed up to apply for the job, was there anything in the facts of the case as you know them and as covered by your testimony which would have negatived such an assumption?''

''Objected to,'' Parma said, ''as being argumentative and calling for a conclusion of the witness; as being not proper cross-examination and assuming facts not in evidence.''

''Sustained,'' Judge Flint said.

Mason, having made his point so that the jurors could get it, smiled at the witness. ''You don't know that the person you were talking with on the telephone was Henrietta Hull, do you?''

''No, sir.''

''Did you ever at any time during the employment call Henrietta Hull?''

''No, sir. She called me.''

''Why didn't you call her?''

''Because she told me not to. She said she would call me.''

''So you were *never* to call her at the house or her place of business?''

''Those were the instructions.''

"Given to you by someone who, for all you know, could have been Dorrie Ambler or any other woman?"

"Objected to as argumentative and not proper cross-examination," Parma said.

"Overruled," Judge Flint said.

"It was only a voice over the telephone," Compton said.

"And from time to time this same voice would call you and give you instructions as to what you were to do?"

"Yes."

"And tell you what instructions you were to give to Dorrie Ambler?"

"Yes."

"You never met the defendant prior to her arrest?"

"No."

"You didn't ever have any conversation with her on the telephone?"

"No."

"You never called the defendant to find out if she had authorized Henrietta Hull to make you any such proposition, and you never called Henrietta Hull?"

"That's right."

"No further questions," Mason said.

Hamilton Burger rose to his feet. "If the Court please," he said, "this next witness will undoubtedly be controversial. I am going to call him somewhat out of order. I am going to state to the Court that I make no apologies for what we have done in granting this witness a certain immunity from prosecution. We —"

"Just a minute," Mason interrupted, getting to his feet, "I submit that this is an improper statement in front of the jury. This is not the time to argue the case, this is not the time to apologize for giving some criminal immunity in order to further the interests of the prosecutor."

"Just a minute, just a minute, gentlemen," Judge Flint interrupted. "I don't want any personalities from either side, and there is no need for any argument. Mr. Burger, if you have another witness, call him."

"Very well," Burger said, turning and smiling at the jury, knowing that he had registered with them the thought that he wished to convey. "Call Dunleavey Jasper."

Dunleavey Jasper was a rather slender young man in his early thirties who managed to convey the impression of slinking as he walked forward, held up his hand, was sworn, and took the witness stand.

"Now, your name is Dunleavey Jasper," Hamilton Burger said. "Where do you reside, Mr. Jasper?"

"In the county jail."

"You are being held there?"

"Yes."

"You are charged with crime?"

"Yes."

"Do you know the defendant?"

"Yes, sir."

"When did you first meet the defendant?"

"It was around the eleventh of September."

"Did you know Dorrie Ambler in her lifetime?"

"Now, just a minute," Judge Flint said. "I've already ruled on this matter. The words, 'in her lifetime,' are

241

extraneous. The jurors are instructed to ignore that part of the question. Now, the question is Mr. Jasper, whether you knew Dorrie Ambler.''

''Yes, sir.''

''How did you get acquainted with Dorrie Ambler?''

''It's rather a long story.''

''Just go ahead and answer the question and never mind how long it takes. Keep your answer responsive to the question but tell how you happened to meet her.''

''She stole my getaway car.''

There was a startled gasp from many of the spectators in the courtroom. The jurors suddenly sat forward in their chairs.

''Will you repeat that, please?'' Hamilton Burger said.

''She stole my getaway car.''

''What was your getaway car?''

''It was a Cadillac automobile, license number WHW 694.''

''This was *your* getaway car?''

''My partner and I were going to use it for a getaway. We didn't have title to the car.''

''Where had you picked up the car?''

''We had stolen it in San Francisco.''

''Who was this partner you refer to?''

''A man named Barlowe Dalton.''

''And you say this was a getaway car.''

''Yes, sir.''

''Where was it when it was taken from you?''

''It was at the Montrose Country Club.''

''And why do you call it a getaway car?''

''Because my partner and I had intended to get in the women's cloakroom, go through the cloaks there, get some fur coats, purses, anything of value we could find, and make a getaway.''

''And what happened?''

''A woman stole our car.''

''Can you explain that?''

''This woman was at the dance. She was intoxicated. She had a fight with her escort and walked out on him, jumped in our getaway car which was standing there with the motor running and drove away.''

''And what did you do after that?''

''Well, there was one thing we had to do. We *had* to find that car.''

''Why?''

''Because we had left something over ten thousand dollars in currency in the glove compartment.''

''And where did this currency come from?''

''We had held up the branch bank in Santa Maria and had taken about eighteen thousand bucks. Ten thousand was wrapped up and was in the glove compartment. The rest of the money we had divided and had on us, about three — four thousand dollars apiece.''

''This was stolen money?''

''That's right.''

''And how about the money that was in the glove compartment? What were the denominations?''

''That was all in one-hundred-dollar bills. The other money we had was in smaller bills, twenties, tens, a few fifties; but there was ten thousand in hundred-dollar bills, and we thought that money might be hot.''

''What do you mean, hot?''

''That perhaps the bank had the serial numbers on it. We had decided to hold it for a while.''

''Go ahead.''

''Well, we had to find the car, so we made inquiries through some of our underworld connections and learned that the car had been involved in a hit and run accident. And then we had a tip that the car was stashed in the garage of Dorrie Ambler, so we found the car but the money was gone. So then we started shadowing Dorrie Ambler.''

''And did you shadow her?'' Burger asked.

''Yes. We had some difficulty picking up her trail but we finally did so and shadowed her for several hours.''

''Where did she go and when?'' Burger asked.

''Objected to as incompetent, irrelevant and immaterial,'' Mason said.

''We'll connect it up, Your Honor,'' Burger said.

"Overruled."

"She went to the office of Perry Mason," the witness said.

"And then?" Burger asked, as the juror leaned forward in tense interest.

"And from there to the airport where she waited until the defendant went into the women's room. At that time she jumped up, approached the newsstand, said, 'This *isn't* a stick-up,' fired a gun three times and ran into the women's room."

"Then what happened?" Burger asked.

"Shortly after that the defendant emerged from the room and was arrested. At first she had us fooled, but there was a difference in voices. So after the police took the defendant away we waited, and sure enough Dorrie Ambler emerged from the rest room. At this time she was wearing a coat which covered her clothes, and dark glasses."

"What did you do then?" Burger asked.

"Followed Dorrie Ambler back to her apartment. By that time we had learned the other woman, the one the police had arrested, was Minerva Minden, an heiress; so we decided we might be on the track of something big.''

''And what did you do then?''

''We waited until the defendant had been released on bail and then we contacted her.''

''By her, you mean the defendant?''

''Right.''

''Both you and Barlowe Dalton contacted her?''

''Yes, sir.''

''Where did you meet her?''

''At a cocktail lounge that she suggested.''

''And what happened there?''

''We had a conversation in which we tried to pin something on her — something that would give us an opening for a shakedown, but she was too smart for us.''

''What do you mean by that?''

''She suggested that we had better go to the police if we thought something was wrong.''

''And then what happened? Go

right ahead.''

''Well, naturally we couldn't afford to have the police nosing around, and what with one thing and another she found out we were a couple of pretty hot torpedoes. The next thing I knew *she* was propositioning *us*.''

''What do you mean by propositioning?''

''She suggested that she wanted to have Dorrie Ambler kidnaped. She offered to pay twenty-five thousand dollars if we'd do the job.''

''Did she say why?''

''Yes.''

''What did she say?''

''She said Dorrie Ambler had seen her pictures in the papers and had decided to cash in on the resemblance by claiming she was the daughter of her mother's sister and that they had the same father, that Dorrie's father was also her father.

''She said Dorrie was clever and that she was trying to bring about some situation where she would be mistaken for the defendant, that some man was backing Dorrie with a lot of money and was trying to make such a spectacular case of it that it would cost her a lot of money to buy Dorrie off.

"So then we told the defendant Dorrie had grabbed off ten grand that belonged to us and that we'd decided to get it back — that she couldn't do that to us, and one thing led to another and finally the defendant asked us if we could get Dorrie — well, out of the picture."

"And what did you and your partner say to that?" Burger asked.

"Well, we said we could if the price was right. Well, she offered us twenty grand and we laughed at her and then she finally came up to fifty grand with five grand additional to cover initial expenses and as a guarantee of good faith on her part."

"Go on," Hamilton Burger said to the witness. "What happened after that?"

"We started making plans."

"Immediately?"

"Yes, sir, that's right — at the time of that same conversation."

"Now, when you say *we* started making plans, whom do you mean?"

"Well, there was the defendant, Minerva Minden, my partner, Barlowe Dalton, and me."

"And what did you do?"

"Well, she gave us the five grand and told us we'd better get busy."

"And what did you do?"

"We went to the Parkhurst Apartments; that is, I did, and cased the joint."

"Now, what do you mean by casing the joint?"

"Well, we looked the place over and made plans for handling things."

"And what did you decide on? What did you actually do?"

"The first thing we did was to get in touch with the manager to see if some apartment on the eighth or ninth floors was vacant. We wanted a close-in place for a base of operations."

"What did you find?"

"I found an apartment on the eighth floor was vacant, 805; that was right close to the stairs and almost directly under Apartment 907 where this Dorrie Ambler had her residence."

"You rented that apartment?"

"Yes, sir. I told the manager that I wanted an apartment, that I thought that 805 would be about right but that I wanted my wife to look at it, that my wife was coming down from San Francisco, that she'd been up with her father who'd been very sick, and she wouldn't be in for a day or so. I suggested that I pay a hundred dollars for a three-day option on the place and that my wife would look at it and if she likcd it, then I'd sign up a lease on it and pay the first and last months' rent."

"What name did you give?"

"The name of William Camas."

"And you were given a key to the apartment on that basis?"

"Yes, sir."

"Then what did you do?"

"Well, it was all fixed up with the defendant that right after the court hearing on her case, which was coming up the next day, she'd rush out to the apartment house and we'd put our plan in operation and get rid of Dorrie Ambler."

"Now you say, 'get rid of her.' Do you mean — Well, what *do* you mean?"

"Well, it eventually turned out we were supposed to get rid of her, but at first the talk was only about kidnaping."

"All right, what happened?"

"Well, you see the defendant was going to come down to join us immediately after her court hearing was finished."

"Did she say *why* she'd picked that particular time?"

"Yes, she said that would be the time when she would be free of shadows and reporters and all that stuff. She said that her attorney would get her out of the court and down in his car and drive her for half a dozen blocks to a place where she had her car parked, that the attorney would give instructions to her to go into hiding and stay in hiding, probably to go home; that she'd come and join us. She said that in case anything should go wrong with our scheme that she could go to the door and impersonate Dorrie Ambler and explain any noise or commotion or anything of that sort. In that way we wouldn't stand any risk."

"All right, what happened?"

"Well, we had a chance to nab Dorrie Ambler while she was in the kitchen. We knocked on the back door and said we had a delivery, and she opened the door and we grabbed her right then."

"What did you do?"

"We put a gag in her mouth, put a gun in her back and hustled her down the back stairs and into Apartment 805. Then we doped her with a shot of morphine and put her out."

"Then what?"

"Shortly after that the defendant showed up. *She* wanted us to get out fast. She said Dorrie Ambler had been consulting Perry Mason and we didn't have much time, that Mason wasn't the sort to let grass grow under his feet. But we reminded her about the ten grand. We really took that apartment to pieces, looking for it."

"Did you find it?"

"No. . . . That is, I don't think we did."

"What do you mean by that?"

"Well, my partner, Barlowe Dalton, acted just a little bit strange. I got to thinking afterwards perhaps he might have found it and just stuck it in his pocket and pretended that he hadn't found it. In that way he'd have had the whole thing for himself instead of making a split."

"You don't know that he found it?"

"No, sir. All I know is that I *didn't* find it."

"Very well. Then what happened?"

"Then I told the defendant we'd better arrange for a getaway in case something went wrong."

"What did you do?"

"I started barricading the kitchen door; that is, the door between the kitchen and the living room so we could open it ourselves but hold off anyone that came in the front door — and that was when the doorbell rang and this man was there."

"What man?"

"This detective, this man that was killed, Marvin Billings."

"All right, go on. Tell us what

happened.''

"Well, I'm getting just a little ahead of my story. The defendant also frisked the apartment looking for something. She didn't tell me what, but she had found a twenty-two-caliber revolver.''

"The defendant had this?''

"That's right. She said she was going to show Dorrie Ambler a thing or two about the difference between lead bullets and blank cartridges.''

"And then?''

"Well, then is when we come to this thing that I was telling you about. The doorbell rang, and this Marvin Billings was there, and the defendant went to the door and tried to shoo him away.''

"What happened?''

"He just pushed his way right into the place and of course right away he saw that it was a wreck, that we'd been searching it, and he wanted to know what was going on. And the defendant, pretending to be Dorrie Ambler, said that somebody had evidently been in looking for something and that was when Billings tried to put the bite on her.''

"Now, what do you mean by that?"

"Well, he wanted to shake her down."

"Where were you?"

"I was in the bedroom."

"Did he see you?"

"No, he couldn't see me. I was behind the door."

"What happened?"

"He told the defendant that he knew what she'd been up to. He thought he was talking to Dorrie —"

"Never mind telling us what you think he thought," Hamilton Burger interrupted with ponderous dignity, creating the impression that he wanted to be thoroughly fair and impartial. "All you can testify is what *you* saw and heard in the presence of the defendant."

"Well, he told her he knew what she'd been up to, that she was an impostor and that she needed a better manager than she had; that he was declaring himself in and that he wanted part of the gravy, and he said something about not being born yesterday, and — Well, that's when she said —"

"Now, when you say 'she,' to whom do you refer?"

"Minerva Minden, the defendant."

"All right, what did she say?"

"She said, 'You may not have been born yesterday but you're not going to live until tomorrow,' and I heard the sound of a shot and then the sound of a body crashing to the floor."

"What did you do?"

"I ran out and said, 'You've shot him!' And she said, 'Of course I've shot him. The blackmailing bastard would have had us all tied up in knots if I hadn't shot him. But they'll never pin it on me. It's in Dorrie Ambler's apartment and she'll get the blame for it.'"

"And then what?"

"Well, then I bent over him and said the guy wasn't even dead, and she said, 'Well, we'll soon fix that,' and raised the gun and then lowered it and a smile came over her face. She said, 'No, better yet, let him recover consciousness long enough to tell his story. He thinks Dorrie Ambler shot him. That will account for Dorrie's disappearance. Everyone will think she shot this guy and then took it on the lam.' ''

''The defendant said that?''

''That's right. And from that time on she was just tickled to death with herself. She was feeling as though she'd really done a job.''

''And what happened?''

''Well, almost immediately after that the chimes rang, and I grabbed the other mattress and rushed it into the kitchen and we arranged a table against the door and the mattresses so that it barricaded the kitchen door. Then we waited a minute to see what would happen. That's when the defendant got in a panic and wanted to run down the stairs. I slapped her and she started to scream. I had to grab her and put a hand over her mouth.''

''Why?'' Hamilton Burger asked.

''Because with someone at the door we couldn't get to the elevator. Our escape was cut off that way. We'd have to go down the stairs. I didn't want them to come around to the back door and catch us there, so I wanted to be sure they were all the way in the apartment before we sneaked out the back door. That tension of waiting was too much for the defendant's nerves.''

''What did you do?''

''I left the back door open.''

''Where was your partner, Barlowe Dalton, at that time?''

''He was down in 805 riding herd on Dorrie Ambler.''

''Go on, what happened?''

''Well, the people at the door turned out to be Perry Mason and this detective, Paul Drake. I waited until they smashed their way into the apartment and had got into the living room, and then the defendant and I slipped out the back door, went down the stairs and holed up in Apartment 805 with Barlowe Dalton and Dorrie Ambler. Dorrie Ambler had been doped and was unconscious by that time.''

''Go on,'' Hamilton Burger said. ''What happened after that?''

''Well, we holed up there. Cops were all over the place and we just sat tight and believe me, I was scared stiff. I told the defendant that if the cops started checking and found us there, it was the gas chamber for all of us, that she'd had no business killing that guy!''

''What did she say?''

''She'd got her nerve back by that time. She laughed and called me chicken and brought out some cards and suggested we play poker.''

''And then what happened?''

''Well, we hung around there until quite late and then the defendant said she'd put on Dorrie Ambler's clothes and go out and see if the coast was clear; that we could watch out the window and if the coast was all clear she'd blink her lights a couple of times on her parked automobile at the curb and that would show us that no cops were around, and we could take Dorrie out.''

''Was Dorrie conscious by that time?''

''She was conscious but groggy. We persuaded her that she wasn't going to get hurt if she did exactly what we told her.''

''So what happened?''

"Well, the defendant went out. She left us a gun — a thirty-eight."

"Did you have any talk with her about what happened after that?"

"Yes, she told me about it the next day."

"What did she say?"

"She said that just as luck would have it, she got in the elevator with some woman and a dog, who was already in the elevator, evidently coming down from one of the upper floors. She said that the woman acted like she knew her but that she turned her back and stood up in front of the elevator door, wondering if the woman was going to speak to her. She said the dog must have known Dorrie Ambler because he got Dorrie Ambler's smell from her clothes and came and pushed his nose against her skirt and leg and wagged his tail. She said it really gave her a bad time."

"And what did she do, of your own knowledge? That is, what do you know?"

"Well, I was looking out of the window of the apartment, and she drove her car around to the designated place and blinked the lights so we knew the coast was clear, so then we took Dorrie Ambler down.''

''And what happened with Miss Ambler?''

''I don't know of my own knowledge, only what Barlowe Dalton told me.''

''You didn't stay with Barlowe Dalton?''

''No, it was understood that he'd take care of Dorrie and that I'd go over the apartment with an oil rag, covering every place where fingerprints might have been left. . . . Incidentally, we'd done that in Dorrie Ambler's apartment as we were searching it. We all wore gloves, and I was going over things with a rag, scrubbing out fingerprints.''

''Now then,'' Hamilton Burger said, ''I'm going to ask you a question which you can answer yes or no. Did Barlowe Dalton tell you what he had done with Dorrie Ambler?''

''Yes.''

''Did you subsequently communicate with the police to tell them what

Barlowe Dalton had told you? Mind you now, I am not asking for hearsay. I am not asking what Barlowe Dalton told you. I am asking you simply what you did.''

''Yes. I communicated with the police.''

''With whom?''

''With Lieutenant Tragg.''

''And what did you tell him? Now, don't say what you actually told him, simply describe what you told him with reference to what Barlowe Dalton had told you.''

''I told him what Barlowe Dalton had told me.''

''Where is Barlowe Dalton now?''

''He is dead.''

''When did he die and how did he die?''

''He died on the twentieth.''

''How did he die?''

''He was killed by a policeman in a holdup.''

Hamilton Burger turned to Perry Mason and bowed. ''You may cross-examine,'' he said.

Minerva Minden grabbed Mason's coat sleeve, pulled herself close to his ear. "That's a pack of lies," she said, "absolute, vicious lies. I never saw this man in my life."

Mason nodded, got to his feet and approached the witness.

"How do you know that Barlowe Dalton is dead?" he asked.

"I saw him killed."

"Where were you?"

"I was standing near him."

"And were you armed at the time?"

"Objected to as not proper cross-examination," Hamilton Burger said. "Incompetent, irrelevant and immaterial."

"Overruled," Judge Flint snapped.

"Were you armed at the time?" Mason asked.

"Yes."

"What did you do with the gun?"

"I dropped it to the floor."

"And the police recovered it?"

"Yes."

"Where was your partner when he was shot?"

"At the Acme Supermarket."

"At what time?"

"About two o'clock in the morning."

"And what were you doing there?"

"Objected to as not proper cross-examination, incompetent, irrelevant and immaterial, calling for matters not covered under direct examination," Hamilton Burger said.

"Overruled," Judge Flint snapped.

"My partner and I were holding up the place."

"Your partner was killed and you were arrested?"

"Yes."

"And you were taken to jail?"

"Yes."

"And how long after you were taken to jail was it that you told the police all you knew about the defendant and Dorrie Ambler?"

"Not very long. You see, my conscience had been bothering me about that murder and about what had happened to Dorrie Ambler. I couldn't get that off my mind."

"How long after the time that you

were arrested did you finally tell the police the complete story?"

"It was — well, it was a couple of days."

"You had been caught red-handed in connection with the perpetration of a burglary."

"Yes, sir."

"You knew that?"

"Yes, sir."

"Have you previously been convicted of a felony?"

"Yes, sir."

"How many times?"

"Three times."

"Of what felony?"

"Armed robbery, grand larceny, burglary."

"You knew that you'd go up for life as an habitual criminal?"

"Just a minute," Hamilton Burger interrupted. "That is objected to as incompetent, irrelevant and immaterial, not proper cross-examination."

"I am simply trying to show the bias and motivation of the witness," Mason said. "I am going to connect it up with my next questions.''

''I think I see the line of your questioning,'' Judge Flint said. ''The objection is overruled.''

''Yes.''

''You knew kidnaping was punishable by death?''

''Under certain circumstances, yes.''

''You knew that you had conspired with the defendant to commit a murder?''

''Yes.''

''As well as a kidnaping?''

''Yes.''

''You knew that you were an accessory after the fact in the murder of Marvin Billings?''

''Well — all right, I suppose I was.''

''And you were in quite a predicament when the authorities were questioning you.''

''Yes, I was.''

''And didn't you finally offer to give them a confession on a crime they were very anxious to solve, if they would give you immunity from prosecution on all of these other charges?''

"Well . . . not exactly."

"What do you mean by that?"

"I mean that they told me that I had better come clean and throw myself on their mercy and — Well they were the ones who said they had the deadwood on me and it would mean that I got life as an habitual criminal and they'd see that I served every minute of it, unless I cooperated and helped them clear up a bunch of unsolved crimes."

"So then the conversation took another turn, didn't it?" Mason said. "You started talking about what would happen to you if you were able to help the officers clear up a murder that they wanted to make a record on."

"Well, something like that."

"You told Lieutenant Tragg that you could clear up some matters for the police if you received immunity for your part in the crime, and if you received immunity for the holdup of the supermarket. Isn't that right?"

"Well, I believe I brought the matter up, yes."

"In other words, you told Lieutenant

Tragg you were willing to make a trade.''

''Not in those words.''

''But that was what it amounted to.''

''Well, yes.''

''And you wanted to be guaranteed immunity before you told your story to the district attorney.''

''Well, that was good business.''

''That's the point I'm getting at,'' Mason said. ''This conscience of yours didn't take over all at once. You decided to do a little bargaining before letting your conscience take over.''

''Well, I wasn't going to tell the police what I knew unless I got immunity. I wasn't going to put my head in a noose just to accommodate them.''

''And *did* you get immunity?''

''I got the promise of immunity.''

''A flat promise of immunity?''

''In a way, yes.''

''Now, just a minute,'' Mason said. ''Let's refresh your recollection. Wasn't it a conditional promise of immunity? Didn't the district attorney say to you in effect that he couldn't give you immunity until he had first heard your story? That if your story resulted in proving a murder and bringing the murderer to justice, that then you would be given immunity provided your testimony was of material help?''

''Well, something like that.''

''That was what you were angling for.''

''Yes.''

''And that's what you got.''

''Yes.''

''So,'' Mason said, leveling his finger at the witness, ''as you sit there on that witness stand, you are charged with a crime which, with your prior record, will probably mean a sentence to life imprisonment, and you have made a bargain with the district attorney that if you can concoct a story which you can tell on this witness stand, which will convince this jury so that they will convict the defendant of first-degree murder, you can walk out of this courtroom scot free and resume your life of crime; but if, on the other hand, your story isn't good enough to convince the jury, then you don't get immunity."

"Now, just a minute, just a minute," Hamilton Burger shouted, getting to his feet. "That question is improper, it calls for a conclusion of the witness, it's argumentative —"

"I think I will sustain the objection," Judge Flint said. "Counsel can ask the question in another way."

"The district attorney told you that if your story resulted in clearing up a murder you might be given immunity?"

"Yes."

"And that he couldn't guarantee you immunity until he had heard your story on the witness stand."

"Not exactly."

"But the understanding was, as he pointed out, that you had to come through with your testimony on the witness stand before you got immunity."

"Well, I had to complete my testimony, yes."

"And it had to result in *clearing up a murder*."

"Yes."

"And bringing the murderer to

justice.''

''Yes.''

''In other words, obtaining a conviction,'' Mason said.

''Well, nobody said that in so many words.''

''I'm saying it in so many words. Look in your own mind. That's the thought that's in the back of your mind right now, isn't it? You want to get this defendant convicted of murder so you can go free of the crimes you committed.''

''I want to get square with myself. I want to tell the truth.''

Mason made a gesture of disgust. ''The truth?'' he exploded. ''You had no intention of telling your story to the police until you were apprehended in the commission of a crime. Isn't that right?''

''Well, I had thought about it.''

''You'd thought about it to this extent,'' Mason said. ''You'd thought about it to the extent of believing that you had an ace trump which you could play when you got into trouble. That you were going to go out and hit the jackpot. You were going on a crime binge; and that in the event you were caught, you would then make a deal with the prosecutor to clean up a murder case in return for immunity.''

''I didn't have any such idea.''

''How many other crimes had you committed during the period between the Dorrie Ambler episode and your attempt to rob the supermarket?''

''I . . . I . . . not any.''

''Wait a minute, wait a minute,'' Mason said. ''Didn't your bargain with the police include the fact that you were going to clean up certain other holdups and clear the record on them?''

''Well, yes.''

''In other words, you were going to confess to all those crimes.''

''Yes.''

''And be given immunity.''

''Yes.''

''Did you or did you not commit those crimes that you were going to confess to?''

''If the Court please,'' Hamilton

273

Burger said, "this cross-examination is entirely improper. The questions are purely for the purpose of degrading the witness in the eyes of the jury and they have no other reason."

"The objection is overruled," Judge Flint said.

"Had you or had you not committed all those crimes that you were going to confess to?" Mason asked. "Crimes that you did confess to."

"I hadn't committed *all* of them, no."

"You had committed *some* of them?"

"Yes."

"And on the other crimes," Mason said, "you were going to tell a lie in order to clear up the records so that the police department could wipe them off the books, with the understanding that you would be given immunity for all those crimes and wouldn't be prosecuted."

"Well, it wasn't exactly like that," the witness said. "They wouldn't buy a pig in a poke. I had to make good first."

"Make good in what way?"

"With my testimony."

"Exactly," Mason said. "If your testimony wasn't strong enough to result in a conviction for this defendant, the deal was off. Isn't that right?"

"I . . . I didn't say it that way."

"You may think you haven't," Mason said, turning on his heel and walking back to his chair. "That's all the cross-examination I have of this witness at this time."

Hamilton Burger, his face flushed and angry, said, "I'll recall Lieutenant Tragg to the stand."

"You have already been sworn, Lieutenant Tragg," Judge Flint said. "Just take the stand."

Tragg nodded, settled himself in the witness chair.

"Lieutenant Tragg," Burger said, "I will ask you if, following a conversation with Dunleavey Jasper, you made a trip to the vicinity of Gray's Well by automobile?"

"I did."

"And what did you look for?"

"I looked for any place where the

automobile road ran within a few feet of a sloping sand dune so constituted that one man could drag a body down the slope of the sand dune.''

''I object, if the Court please,'' Mason said, ''to the last part of the witness' statement as a conclusion of the witness, not responsive to the question and having no bearing on the facts of the case as we have those facts at present.''

''The objection is sustained. The last part of the answer will go out,'' Judge Flint said.

''And what did you find?'' Hamilton Burger asked, smiling slightly at the knowledge he had got his point across to the jury.

''After three or four false leads, we found a sand hill where there were faint indications that something had disturbed the surface of the sand, and by following those indications to the bottom of the sand hill and digging we found the badly decomposed body of a woman.''

''Were you able to identify that body?''

''Objected to as incompetent,

irrelevant and immaterial,'' Mason said.

''The objection is overruled. This evidence, ladies and gentlemen of the jury, is being admitted purely for the purpose of corroborating the testimony of the previous witness and not with the idea that any less evidence would be required in the case at bar because there might be evidence indicating the possible commission of another crime. Nor are you to permit yourselves to consider any subsequent crime, even for the purpose of proving motivation, but only for the purpose of corroborating the testimony of the previous witness. You are to consider this evidence only for that limited purpose. Continue, Mr. Prosecutor.''

''I will ask you this, Lieutenant Tragg. Was there anything anywhere on the body that gave any clue as to its identity?''

''There was.''

''Will you describe it, please?''

''The tips of the fingers were badly decomposed. The weather had been intensely hot. The body had been buried in a rather shallow sand grave. Putrefaction and an advanced stage of decomposition make it difficult to make a positive identification. However, by a process of pickling the fingers in a formaldehyde solution and hardening them, we were able to get a fairly good set of fingerprints sufficient to give certain aspects of identification.''

''Now then, Lieutenant Tragg, I will ask you if you made prints of the thumbs of this body.''

''We did. We printed all the fingers as best we could.''

''I am at the moment particularly interested in the thumbs. I am going to ask you if you found any other physical evidence on the body.''

''We did.''

''What did you find?''

''We found a purse, and in that purse we found a receipt for rent of Apartment 907 at the Parkhurst Apartments. That receipt was made out in the name of Dorrie Ambler. We also found a key to Apartment 907. We found some other receipts made to Dorrie Ambler.''

"Did you find a driving license made to Dorrie Ambler?"

"Not there."

"Please pay attention to my question, Lieutenant. I didn't ask you that question. I asked you if you found a driving license made out to Dorrie Ambler."

"We did."

"Where did you find that?"

"That driving license was in the possession of the defendant at the time of her arrest. It was tucked down in a concealed pocket in her purse."

"And did that driving license contain the thumbprint of the applicant?"

"It contained a photostat of it."

"And did you subsequently attempt to compare the thumbprint of the cadaver you discovered with the thumbprint on the driving license of Dorrie Ambler?"

"I did."

"With what result?"

"Objected to as calling for a conclusion of the witness," Mason said. "It is incompetent, irrelevant and immaterial. It is not the best evidence.

The jury are entitled to have the thumbprints presented to them for comparison, and Lieutenant Tragg can, if he wishes, point out points of similarity in the prints. But he cannot testify to his conclusion.''

''I think I will sustain the objection,'' Judge Flint said.

''Very well. It will prolong the case,'' Hamilton Burger said.

''In a case of this magnitude the time element is not particularly essential, Mr. Prosecutor,'' Judge Flint rebuked.

Hamilton Burger bowed gravely.

He introduced a photographic enlargement of the thumbprint of Dorrie Ambler, taken from her application for a driving license. Then he introduced a photograph of the thumbprint of the woman whose body Lieutenant Tragg had found.

''Now then, Lieutenant Tragg,'' Hamilton Burger said, ''by pointing to these two enlarged photographs which are on easels standing where the jurors can see them, can you point out any similarities?''

"I can. I have listed the points of similarity."

"How many do you find?"

"I find six."

"Will you point them out to the jury, please? Take this pointer and point to them on the easels."

Lt. Tragg pointed out the various points of similarity.

"And these are all?" Hamilton Burger asked.

"No, sir. They are not all. They are the only ones that I can be sufficiently positive of to make a complete identification. You will realize that due to the process of putrefaction and decomposition it was exceedingly difficult to get a good legible fingerprint from the body of the deceased. We did the best we could, that's all."

"Were you able to form an opinion as to the age and sex of the decedent?"

"Oh, yes. The body was that of a female, apparently in the early twenties."

"And you took specimens of hair from the body?"

"We did. And those were compared with the hair color of Dorrie Ambler as mentioned in the application for driving license."

"Did you find anything else at or near the body of this woman?" Hamilton Burger asked.

"We found a thirty-eight-caliber revolver with one discharged shell and five loaded shells. It was a Smith and Wesson with a two-inch barrel, Number C-48809."

"Did you subsequently make tests with that gun in the ballistics department?"

"I did."

"You fired test bullets through it?"

"Yes, sir."

"And did you make a comparison with any other bullet?"

"Yes, sir."

"What bullet?"

"A bullet that had been recovered from the skull of the body I found there in the sand hills."

"And what did you find?"

"The bullets showed identical

striations. The bullets had been fired from the same gun; that is, the fatal bullet matched absolutely with the test bullets.''

''Do you have photographs showing the result of the experiments?''

''I do.''

''Will you present them, please?''

Lt. Tragg presented photographs of the fatal bullet and the test bullet.

''What is this line of demarcation in the middle?''

''That is a line of demarcation made in a comparison microscope. The bullet above that line is the fatal bullet; the bullet below is the test bullet.''

''And those bullets are rotated on this comparison microscope until you reach a point where the lines of identity coincide? Where the striations are continuations of each other?''

''Yes, sir.''

''And when that happens, what does it indicate, Lieutenant?''

''That the bullets were both fired from the same gun.''

''And that is the case here?''

"Yes, sir."

"You may cross-examine," Hamilton Burger said abruptly.

Mason approached the witness. "Lieutenant Tragg, was the body you discovered that of Dorrie Ambler? Please answer that question yes or no."

Lt. Tragg hesitated. "I think it —"

"I don't want to know what you *think*," Mason interrupted. "I want to know what you *know*. Was the body that of Dorrie Ambler or not?"

"I don't know," Tragg said.

"You didn't get enough points of similarity from the fingerprint to establish identification?"

"I will state this," Lt. Tragg said, "we got enough points of identification to show a very strong probability."

"But you can't establish it by definite proof as to identification?"

"Well . . ."

"Be frank, Lieutenant," Mason interrupted. "It takes a minimum of twelve points of identity to establish positive identification, does it not?"

"Well, no, it does not," Tragg said.

284

"We have had rather a large number of cases where we were able to make identification from fewer points of identity."

"How many?"

"Well, in some instances, nine or ten points are sufficient where the circumstances are such that we can negative the possibility of accidental duplication."

"But those circumstances didn't exist in this case?"

"No."

"You don't consider that six points of similarity are sufficient to prove identity."

"Not by themselves. There are, of course, other matters. When you consider the probabilities of six points of similarity in the fingerprints where it was impossible to obtain a completely legible impression; when you consider rental receipts in the name of Dorrie Ambler; when you consider the key to the apartment being found in the purse of the decedent; when you consider the age, the sex, the size, the coloration of the hair, and group all those together, we can determine a very strong mathematical probability.''

''Exactly,'' Mason said. ''You have a strong mathematical probability of identity. Yet you can't testify that the body was that of Dorrie Ambler.''

''I can't swear to it positively, no, sir.''

''Now, you talk about the mathematical probabilities of sex, among other things,'' Mason said. ''Sex alone would be of poor probative value, would it not?''

''Well, yes.''

''Now, the similarity of six points of identification would not prove the fingerprints were identical?''

''No, I have explained that. However, I can list the probabilities in this way. The identity of the six points of similarity would give us, I would say, about one chance in fifty that the body was not that of Dorrie Ambler. The presence of the key to the apartment makes another mathematical factor. There are hundreds of apartment houses in Los Angeles. In the apartment house in question there are ten floors. Each has thirty apartments, and the fact that the key to Apartment 907 was found would then be one in three hundred, and multiplying one in three hundred by fifty we have a factor of one in fifteen thousand, and —"

"Now, just a minute," Mason interrupted. "You are not qualifying as an expert mathematician, Lieutenant Tragg."

"Well, I'm an expert in the field of criminal investigation and I can make the ordinary mathematical computations."

"Exactly," Mason said, "and you can twist them so that you can come up with a perfectly astronomical figure when it suits your purpose.

"We could, for instance, go at it this way. You could say that there are only two sexes; therefore the fact that the decedent was a female gives us a one out of two chance; that there are only one-tenth of adult females within the age bracket you were able to determine; that therefore you have a factor of twenty to one that this was the person in question; that of the persons in that age group only approximately one in twenty have that coloration of hair so you can multiply and get a factor of four hundred to one; and —''

''Now, that's not fair,'' Lt. Tragg interrupted. ''That's distorting the facts.''

''But it's following the same line of reasoning that you use in trying to establish a mathematical law of probabilities,'' Mason said. ''I'm going to put it to you just this way. You can't state beyond a reasonable doubt that the body was that of Dorrie Ambler, can you?''

''No.''

''That's all,'' Mason said.

''Now I wish to call one more witness, perhaps out of order,'' Hamilton Burger said. ''I wish to call Rosy Chester.''

Rosy Chester, a red-haired, rather voluptuous woman with a hard, cynical mouth and alert eyes, came forward and was sworn.

"Where is your residence?" Hamilton Burger asked.

"At the present time in the county jail."

"Are you acquainted with the defendant?"

"I am."

"When did you first meet the defendant?"

"We were cell mates for a night."

"On that occasion did you have any discussion with this defendant about Dorrie Ambler?"

"Yes."

"What, if anything, did the defendant say about her?"

"The defendant said that Dorrie Ambler would never be seen again."

"Was there any further conversation?" Burger asked.

"I asked her if she wasn't worried that Dorrie Ambler could collect a share of the estate, and she laughed and said Dorrie Ambler would never show up to claim any share of any estate."

"Do you know whether this was

before or after the body had been discovered?''

''I think the body had been discovered, but the defendant didn't know about it. It hadn't been announced publicly.''

''Cross-examine,'' Hamilton Burger said.

''Are you awaiting trial on some charge?'' Mason asked.

''Yes.''

''What?''

''Possession of marijuana.''

''As soon as you had this conversation with the defendant you communicated with the prosecutor?''

''Shortly afterwards.''

''How did you reach him?''

''He reached me.''

''Oh,'' Mason said, ''then you were told that you were going to be put in the same cell with the defendant and to try to get her to talk?''

''Something like that.''

''And you did try to get her to talk?''

''Well — Of course when you're together in a cell that way you don't have much to talk about and —"

"Did you or did you not try to get her to talk?"

"Well . . . yes."

"And tried to lead her into making some incriminating statement?"

"I tried to get her to talk."

"Under instructions from the district attorney?" Mason asked.

"Yes."

"And why did you take it on yourself to act as a source of information for the district attorney?"

"He asked me to."

"And what did he tell you he would do if you were successful?"

"He didn't tell me anything."

"He didn't make you any promises?"

"Absolutely not."

"Now then," Mason said, "what did he say about the fact that he couldn't make you any promises?"

"Oh," she said, "he told me that if he made any promises to me that that would impair the weight of my testimony so that I'd just have to trust his sense of gratitude."

Mason smiled and turned to the jury. "That," he said, is all."

Hamilton Burger flushed, said, "That's all."

Judge Flint said, "Court will now take a recess until tomorrow morning at nine-thirty A.M. During that time the defendant will be remanded to custody, and the jurors will not discuss the case among themselves or permit it to be discussed in their presence or form or express any opinion as to the guilt or innocence of the defendant."

Judge Flint arose and left the bench.

Minerva Minden clutched Mason's arm.

"Mr. Mason," she said, "I have a confession to make."

"No, you haven't," Mason told her.

"I do, I do. You *must* know something, you simply *must*. Otherwise I'll . . . I'll be convicted of a murder I didn't do."

Mason's eyes met hers. "I'm going to tell you something that I very seldom tell a client," he said. "Shut up. Don't talk to me. Don't tell me anything. I

292

don't want to know anything about the facts of the case.''

''But, Mr. Mason, if you don't know, they'll — Can't you see, the evidence against me is overwhelming? They'll convict me of a murder that —''

''Shut up,'' Mason said. ''Don't talk to me and I don't want to talk with you.''

Mason got to his feet and motioned the policewoman.

Mason said as a parting shot to his client, ''Don't discuss this case with *anybody*. I don't want you to answer *any* questions. I want you to sit absolutely tight. Say nothing, not a word.''

Chapter Thirteen

Back in his office, Mason paced the floor while Della Street watched him with anxious eyes.

"Can you tell me what's worrying you, Chief?" she asked.

Mason said, "It's a tricky situation, Della. I've got to handle it in just the right way. If I do *exactly* the right thing and say *exactly* the right thing at *exactly* the right time, that's one thing. If I misplay my cards, it's another."

Abruptly Mason stopped in his pacing. "Della," he said, "get Paul Drake on the line, tell him I want to know every circumstance connected with the holdup of the bank at Santa Maria."

"Is that pertinent?" Della Street asked.

"That's pertinent," Mason said. "Tell Paul I want a complete report listing every circumstance, every bit of evidence. Nothing is too minute, nothing is to be discarded.

"Have him charter a plane, fly an operative up there. Get busy. Work with witnesses."

"You want the report by morning?" Della Street asked.

"I want the operative who makes the investigation to be back here by morning," Mason said. "I want him in the courtroom where I can talk with him. Tell Paul to spare no expense, to charter a plane.

"Also tell Paul I want a complete report of all unsolved stick-ups between San Francisco and Los Angeles on the fifth, sixth and seventh of September. He can start collecting those by long distance telephone.

"Have him call police chiefs at the various cities. I want everything I can get."

"But, look here," Della Street said, "you can't get around Jasper's testimony about the gun, the conversations and the place where the body was found unless you —"

"All that testimony isn't going to hurt the defendant," Mason said.

"What!" she exclaimed.

"The murder of Dorrie Ambler doesn't mean anything in *this* case," Mason said, "unless the jury believes Minerva *told* them to murder her. If I can open up a doubt on that one point, then I can blast Jasper's testimony. The death of Dorrie Ambler doesn't mean a thing unless Minerva Minden *told* them to kill her.

"Even if Minerva Minden had an argument with Dorrie Ambler and killed her in the heat of passion, it wouldn't have anything to do with *this* case unless it corroborated Jasper's testimony, and if he is lying about being told to murder Dorrie Ambler, then he could be lying about the murder of Billings."

Della Street shook her head. "You could never get a jury to believe that. They'd convict Minerva anyway."

"If I play this right," Mason said,

"the judge is going to have to instruct the jury to return a verdict of not guilty."

"He'd never dare to do that on a technicality," Della Street said.

"Want to bet?" Mason asked.

Chapter Fourteen

Hamilton Burger was on his feet as soon as court had convened the next morning and Judge Flint had taken the bench.

"If the Court please," he said, "in the case of the People of the State of California versus Minerva Minden I have one more piece of evidence to put in. I have here a certified copy of the firearms register showing the purchase by Minerva Minden of a thirty-eight-caliber Smith and Wesson revolver, Number C-48809.

"This is a sales record kept in accordance with law and is, I believe, prima-facie evidence of the matters therein contained. I offer this in evidence."

"We have no objection," Mason said.

"The matter may go in."

Paul Drake, accompanied by Jerry Nelson, hurriedly entered the courtroom, caught Mason's eye.

The lawyer said, "May I have the indulgence of the Court for a moment, please?" and as Judge Flint nodded, Mason moved over to join the detectives.

Drake said in a low voice, "Nelson has all that's known on that Santa Maria bank job, Perry. There were three persons on it, two in the bank, one driving the getaway car. Witnesses got a partial license number and description. It's the same car as the hit-and-run car and —"

"The driver," Mason interrupted. "Was it a woman?"

Drake's face showed surprise. "How did you know? Yes, it was a woman."

"Any other jobs?" Mason asked.

"Yes, a liquor store stick-up in Bakersfield. It's probably the same gang again — a light-colored Cadillac and a woman getaway driver."

"Thanks," Mason said. "That's

all I need.''

He turned to face Judge Flint. ''If the Court please, before the prosecutor calls his next witness I have a question or two in regard to fingerprints which I would like to ask of Lieutenant Tragg on cross-examination. I notice that he is here in court and I ask the Court to be permitted to resume my cross-examination of this witness.''

''Is there any objection?'' Judge Flint asked.

''There is, if the Court please,'' Hamilton Burger said. ''I think defense counsel should cross-examine his witnesses and complete his cross-examination. It is a habit of counsel to conduct piecemeal cross-examinations and —''

''The sequence of proof on all matters of procedure in connection with the examination of a witness are in the exclusive control of the Court,'' Judge Flint said. ''The Court in this case is particularly anxious to see that the defendant is not foreclosed in any manner from presenting her defense.

"The Court has decided to permit the motion. Lieutenant Tragg will return to the stand for further cross-examination."

As Tragg stepped forward Mason nodded to Della Street, who opened a leather case, took out a folding tripod, placed it in front of the witness, put a small projector on the tripod, ran an electrical connection to a socket and put up a screen.

"This is to be a demonstration?" Judge Flint asked.

"I simply want to project a fingerprint so that I can get it to an exact size," Mason said, "and question Lieutenant Tragg concerning points of similarity."

"Very well, proceed."

Mason turned on the projector, experimented for a moment with a spot of light on the screen, then said, "Now, Lieutenant, I am going to take a print of the thumb of the defendant on this specially prepared glass slide."

Mason went over, extended his hand and Minerva Minden put out her thumb. Mason pressed the thumb against the slide for a moment, then said apologetically to the Court, "I may have to repeat this experiment, if the Court please, because I am not an expert in taking fingerprints."

He went to the projector, put in the slide, focused it for a moment, said, "I am afraid I have smudged this one."

He took another slide from his pocket, again went to the defendant, again received a thumbprint, then returned to the projector and focused the lens on the screen.

"Ah, yes," Mason said, "we're getting it now. I think this thumbprint is clear enough. You can see that, can you, Lieutenant?"

"Very well," Lt. Tragg said.

"All right, I'll arrange it so the three prints are as nearly the same size as possible; that is, the print on the left, which is the thumbprint of Dorrie Ambler; the print on the right of that which is the print of the thumb of the dead woman; and over on the right of that again, this print which I am projecting."

"Now, just a minute," Hamilton

Burger said, getting to his feet. "This is simply a projection, and evanescent bit of evidence which we can't identify. The other prints are enlarged photographs which can be introduced in evidence."

"Well," Mason said, "you can have this slide introduced in evidence, put in an envelope and marked an appropriate exhibit."

"Very well," Hamilton Burger said, "if that's the best we can do. I should prefer a photograph."

"It depends somewhat on the point counsel is trying to make," Judge Flint said.

Mason said, "I am trying to test the qualifications of this witness, and to show the fallacy of an identification made from only six points of similarity."

"Very well," Judge Flint said, "proceed with your questioning, and when you have finished, this slide can be put in an envelope, marked for identification and then introduced as an exhibit if either side desires."

"Now then, Lieutenant," Mason said,

"these prints are all about the same size. Now, I am going to call your attention to this projected print and ask you if you can find points of similarity between that and the print of the dead girl."

"There should be some points of similarity," Lt. Tragg said, "and there might be several, depending upon certain similarities of design."

"Well, just approach the exhibits and indicate with a pointer any points of similarity you can find."

"Well, here's one, to start with," Lt. Tragg said. "They have almost identical whorl patterns in the center."

"All right, proceed."

"Now, here's a junction . . ."

"Go right ahead, Lieutenant."

Tragg looked at the fingerprints thoughtfully, then said, "I'll just trace out these points of similarity, if I may, because once the projection is removed from the paper, there will be nothing to indicate what points of similarity I was referring to."

"That's quite all right. Go right ahead," Mason said. "There's a sheet

304

of white paper on which I am projecting this fingerprint and you may make tracings of any of the points of similarity which you discover.''

Lt. Tragg took a pen from his pocket, traced lines, studied the print, made more tracings and finally after some five minutes backed away from the print.

''Any more points of similarity?'' Mason asked.

''No,'' Tragg said, ''I see none at the moment.''

''Now, how many points of similarity have you discovered, Lieutenant?''

''Six,'' Lt. Tragg said.

''The exact number that you had discovered with the print of Dorrie Ambler,'' Mason said. ''I think, Lieutenant, that is rather a graphic and dramatic demonstration of the fact that an absolute identification cannot be made from six points of similarity. You have now established that this defendant is the dead woman you discovered.''

Lt. Tragg studied the two fingerprints with frowning concentration for a moment, then returned to the witness stand.

"I have no further questions," Mason said.

"No redirect examination on this point," Hamilton Burger said. "The witness said earlier that six points of similarity did *not* necessarily prove identity."

"That's all. You may leave the stand," Judge Flint said.

Mason switched out the light in the projector, removed the slide and said, "Now, I believe the Court instructed that this slide was to be placed in an envelope and marked for identification."

Mason put the slide in an envelope and handed it to the clerk.

Hamilton Burger thoughtfully studied the tracings of lines which had been made by Lt. Tragg on the white paper underneath the projected fingerprints. He beckoned to Lt. Tragg, and Tragg, on his way from the witness stand, paused to confer in whispers with the prosecutor.

Now that the projection had been removed, the six points which Lt. Tragg had traced on the white paper showed out with startling clarity.

Suddenly Hamilton Burger pushed Lt. Tragg back, jumped to his feet, said, "Just a moment, Lieutenant. Return to the stand. Now, Your Honor, I do have some questions on redirect and I want to get this envelope from the clerk. I want that projection to be put on the white paper screen once more."

"I'll be only too glad to accommodate the prosecutor," Mason said.

"You keep your hands off that envelope," Hamilton Burger shouted. "I want someone to take that envelope, that very identical envelope right there, which you have just had marked for identification. I don't want any hocus-pocus here."

"I think that insinuation is uncalled for, Mr. Prosecutor," Judge Flint said in an acrid rebuke.

"You just wait a moment," Hamilton Burger said, his voice so excited that it was hard for him to control it. "Just wait a moment and see if it's an unjustified criticism. Look at that paper

307

screen with the marks on it and then look at the photograph of the fingerprint of Dorrie Ambler.

"Not only did Lieutenant Tragg find six points of similarity between the projected print and the print of the dead woman, *but they're exactly the same points of similarity as shown on the Dorrie Ambler fingerprint.*"

"I'm afraid I don't understand," Judge Flint said.

"Well, I understand," Hamilton Burger said. "That print that was projected on the screen wasn't the fingerprint of the defendant at all. Perry Mason took her thumbprint, pretended that it had been smeared, went back to take another print and that gave him an opportunity to juggle slides. The fingerprint he projected on the screen wasn't the fingerprint of the defendant at all but was a fingerprint of Dorrie Ambler which he had managed to have made into a slide by some photographic process which would duplicate the appearance of a freshly made fingerprint."

"Are you making this as a charge, Mr. Burger?"

"I'm making it as an accusation and I demand that Mr. Mason be searched. I want that other slide taken from his pocket before he has a chance to destroy it. This is a fraud upon the Court, it is an attempt to conceal evidence, it is a criminal conspiracy and unprofessional conduct."

"Now, just a minute," Judge Flint said. "We're going to go at this in an orderly manner. Mr. Clerk, you will put that slide back in the projector. Mr. Mason, you will stand right here, please, and the Court is going to ask you to take the other slide from your pocket, the one that you said was smeared, and hand it to the Court."

Mason put his hand in his pocket, handed a slide to the Court.

"Now then," Judge Flint said, "let's have that slide which was marked for identification put back on the screen."

Hamilton Burger, intensely excited, said, "I want it just the same size as it was. It can be matched by the markings made by Lieutenant Tragg on the screen.''

''We'll have it the same size,'' Judge Flint said. ''There's no reason to shout, Mr. Burger. I can hear you perfectly.''

The clerk focused the projector.

''Move that projector back just a little,'' Hamilton Burger said, ''just an inch or so. Get the marks so they coincide with the tracings made by Lieutenant Tragg . . . there we are.''

Hamilton Burger turned to Lt. Tragg.

''Now, Lieutenant,'' he said, ''forget all about the print of the dead woman. Look at the projected print and the photographic print of Dorrie Ambler and tell me how many points of similarity you find in *those* prints!''

Lt. Tragg said, ''I will take a pointer and —''

''Here, take this red crayon,'' Hamilton Burger said. ''Mark the points of similarity with the red crayon. Let's see how many points of similarity you find between the projected print and that of Dorrie Ambler.''

Lt. Tragg went to the exhibits, started

tracing ridges with red crayon. After some few minutes he said, "I have already found more than eighteen points of similarity, if the Court please. Twelve points of similarity are sufficient to make an absolute identification."

"And that means?" Judge Flint asked.

"It means that the projected print is not the print of the defendant at all but is the print of Dorrie Ambler."

"You're absolutely certain of that?" Judge Flint asked.

"Absolutely certain."

Judge Flint turned to Perry Mason. "Mr. Mason," he said, "you stand charged before this Court with a very grave offense, an offense which could well lead to disciplinary action or disbarment proceedings. It would certainly lead to a charge of contempt of Court. I am going to ask you to plead on the charge of contempt of Court right here and right now.

"In view of the fact that this matter came up while the jury was present, I am going to have it determined while the jury is present. Now then, Mr. Mason, I am going to ask you how it happened that in pretending to take an imprint of the defendant's thumb you substituted a slide with the imprint of Dorrie Ambler.''

Mason said, ''I am sorry, Your Honor, I have no explanation.''

''In that event,'' Judge Flint said, ''the Court is going to —''

''May I make one statement?''

''Very well,'' Judge Flint snapped. ''Make a statement.''

''I simply suggest,'' Mason said, ''that in order to avoid any confusion, the witness, Lieutenant Tragg, take a fingerprint of the defendant's thumb. Then we will project that on the screen and Lieutenant Tragg can see how many points of similarity he finds between that and the print of the dead woman. In that way there can be no question of confusion. I have here an acetate slide coated with a substance which will show the fingerprint characteristics.''

Judge Flint hesitated.

''I would like very much to have that done,'' Hamilton Burger said.

"Very well. You may proceed," Judge Flint said.

Mason handed a slide to Lt. Tragg who inspected it carefully, took a magnifying glass from his pocket, looked at it, then approached the defendant, took her thumbprint, returned to the projector, removed the slide which was in the projector and inserted the slide of the thumbprint he had just taken.

"Now then," Mason said, "perhaps the Lieutenant will be good enough to tell us how many points of similarity there are between *that* fingerprint, the fingerprint of the dead woman and the fingerprint of Dorrie Ambler."

Lt. Tragg adjusted the focus just right, then approached the projected print.

Suddenly he stopped.

"They coincide," he said.

"What coincides?" Hamilton Burger snapped at him.

"The points of similarity which I have traced on the paper in red and in green coincide with the pattern now projected on the screen."

Hamilton Burger said, "Well — They can't."

"But they do," Mason said. "It's quite evident. The Court can see for itself, and the jurors can see the same thing."

"Now, just one moment!" Hamilton Burger shouted. "Here's some more hocus-pocus. I insist that we have this phase of the matter disposed of in the absence of the jury."

"We've had the rest of it in the presence of the jury," Judge Flint said. "I think we'll clear up this entire situation in the presence of the jury. . . . Now Lieutenant, exactly what is the meaning of this?"

"I don't know," Lt. Tragg said.

"I suggest," Mason said, "that it means the projected fingerprint which I put on the screen *was* the fingerprint of the defendant and that the prosecutor's charge that I had juggled slides, the prosecutor's charge that I had substituted fingerprints and all of his remarks concerning misconduct, were unjustified, were accusations made in the presence of the jury and constituted misconduct on the part of the prosecutor.''

''Now, let's get this straight,'' Judge Flint said. ''Lieutenant, look up here. Now, Lieutenant, is it true that there are eighteen points of similarity between the fingerprint of the defendant and the fingerprint of Dorrie Ambler?''

''Yes, Your Honor.''

''How could that happen, Lieutenant? You have just testified under oath that twelve points of similarity would show an absolute indentification; yet you have here eighteen points of similarity between the prints of two different people.''

''I'm afraid,'' Lt. Tragg said, ''that there's something here I don't understand. I have now noticed more points of similarity. I could go on and probably get many other points of similarity.''

''And what does that mean?'' Judge Flint asked.

''It means,'' Perry Mason said dryly, ''that either the science of fingerprinting is breaking down or that this defendant

315

and Dorrie Ambler are one and the same person, in which event there never was any Dorrie Ambler and the testimony of the witness, Dunleavey Jasper, that he saw the two women together and noticed their similarity is absolute perjury.

"The Court will notice that other witnesses have testified to the similarity of appearance of Dorrie Ambler on the one hand and the defendant on the other, but no witness has been produced who had seen them together, and no witness could be produced who had seen them together because there was only one person. Therefore the testimony of Dunleavey Jasper that he saw them together is —"

Judge Flint shouted, "Bailiff, apprehend that man! Keep him from leaving the courtroom."

Dunleavey Jasper, halfway through the swinging door was grabbed by the bailiff. He turned and engaged in a frantic struggle.

The courtroom was in an uproar.

Judge Flint shouted, "The spectators

will be seated! The jurors will be seated! Court will take a fifteen-minute recess.''

Chapter Fifteen

As court was reconvened amidst the breathless hush of excitement, Mason got to his feet. "If the Court please," he said, "it appearing that there never was any such person as Dorrie Ambler, and in view of the fact that the prosecutor now knows a confession of perjury has been obtained from Dunleavey Jasper, I move the Court to instruct the jury to return a verdict of not guilty and discharge the defendant from custody."

"Does the prosecutor have any statement?" Judge Flint asked.

Hamilton Burger dejectedly got to his feet.

"I don't understand it, Your Honor," he said, "and I think that the patience of the Court has been imposed upon by reason of the fact that the defense did not disclose this matter to the Court at an earlier date but chose to present it in this dramatic manner. However, that is a matter for the Court to take up with counsel for the defense. As far as the present motion is concerned, I will verify the fact that Dunleavey Jasper has made a confession.''

''I think,'' Judge Flint said, ''that it would clarify matters if the general substance of that confession were a part of the record. Would you care to make a statement, Mr. Prosecutor?''

''It seems,'' Burger said, ''that Dunleavey Jasper, Barlowe Dalton, and a young woman named Flossie Hendon, stole this Cadillac car and started south.

''These people had committed various crimes before they stole the Cadillac. Afterwards they committed other crimes, among them the holdup of the branch bank at Santa Maria where they secured some eighteen thousand dollars. They divided eight thousand dollars of this money into three equal lots, and the balance of ten thousand dollars was wrapped in paper, held in place with rubber bands, and placed in the glove compartment of the stolen automobile.

"They went to the Montrose Country Club intending to steal valuable furs from the cloakroom, to hold up the cashier for the large sum of money which they thought would be in the safe that evening. They left their getaway car with Flossie Hendon at the wheel, and she was supposed to be there with the motor running, ready to help them escape as soon as they had completed their crime.

"However, Flossie Hendon succumbed to the feminine urge to look in at the gowns of the dancers who were in the country club. She left the wheel of the car for only a few moments but that was long enough.

"Minerva Minden had apparently forfeited her driving license for drunk driving some months earlier. So that she wouldn't be deprived of the privilege of driving a car, she had established a dual identity, taking the name of Dorrie Ambler and renting the apartment in the

Parkhurst Apartments, staying there on occasion and building up a bona fide identity so in case the validity of this second driving license should ever be questioned she could have proof of her identity.

"Since the attendant at the parking lot saw she was under the influence of liquor and asked to see her driving license, she showed him the only one she had — the one made out to Dorrie Ambler.

"Later on, she had an argument with her escort, ran blindly out of the club seeking a taxicab. She saw the stolen Cadillac with the motor running, jumped in and took off, driving to her apartment.

"We can only surmise what happened. Presumably she became involved in a hit-and-run accident, put the car in the garage at the Parkhurst Apartments and from there on the situation seems to have been deliberately obscured in order to keep the police from involving her in another accident involving drunken driving, which would have resulted in the revocation of her probation and the imposition of a long jail sentence.

"Quite naturally the three criminals wished to recover the stolen automobile since there was ten thousand dollars in the glove compartment. They traced the automobile to Dorrie Ambler, through the parking lot attendent, eventually traced Dorrie Ambler to the Parkhurst Apartments, and went there to search the apartment after having rented Apartment 805 as a base. While they were there in Apartment 907, Marvin Billings caught them red-handed. Barlowe Dalton shot him with the twenty-two-caliber revolver they had found in the apartment where they had also found the thirty-eight revolver.

"It was at that time that Perry Mason and Paul Drake came to the door of the apartment.

"Subsequently, after having made their escape by barricading the door to the kitchen and going down the service stairs to Apartment 805, which they had rented for the purpose of giving them a base of operations, the two men read in the paper about Perry Mason's connection with the case and the similarity of identities, and came to the conclusion that either Dorrie Ambler or Minerva Minden had found their stolen ten thousand dollars.

"At about that time Flossie Hendon, a young delinquent who had gone with the two hoodlums on their career of crime for kicks, as she expressed it, was quite concerned about the murder of Marvin Billings. Murder was more than she had bargained for.

"So Jasper says his partner, Barlowe Dalton, was the one who took her for a ride, killed her with the thirty-eight they had stolen from the apartment in the Parkhurst Apartments. Of course now that Dalton is dead, Jasper glibly puts all the murders on his shoulders.

"Later on, when Jasper was apprehended in a burglary where Barlowe Dalton had been killed, Jasper conceived the idea of getting immunity for himself by means of confessing to the kidnaping of Dorrie Ambler and involving Minerva Minden.

"Flossie Hendon had been murdered to keep her from talking. Apparently the body which was discovered, the badly decomposed body, was that of Flossie Hendon, and Jasper shrewdly counted on advanced putrefaction to make positive identification impossible.

"In the meantime the defendant, going to the apartment she had rented under the name of Dorrie Ambler, learned of the murder and left the building in a state of some excitement. It was at that time she was seen by the witness."

Hamilton Burger paused, then said, "If the Court please, I dislike to make this confession, but there are times when we who are prosecutors have to rely upon the evidence as it comes to us and have to use our judgment.

"We felt that Dunleavey Jasper was telling the truth. We were willing to give him immunity on a relatively minor crime in order to convict a murderess. The fact that things didn't work out that way, the fact that we were victimized, is one of the hazards of law enforcement.

"I have made this statement so that the record may be cleared. We are going to proceed against Dunleavey Jasper for the crimes he has admitted, and I think we will proceed against him for murder, both the murder of Marvin Billings and the murder of Flossie Hendon."

Hamilton Burger, with what dignity he could muster, turned and stalked from the courtroom, leaving to his associates the unpleasant task of remaining through the final stages of the case.

Judge Flint said, "The jurors will be instructed to return a verdict of not guilty in this case of the People of the State of California versus Minerva Minden."

Chapter Sixteen

Mason, Della Street and Paul Drake sat in the lawyer's office.

"When," Della Street asked, "did you realize there weren't two women?"

"When Minny Minden showed us there was no scar on her abdomen," Mason said.

Della Street glanced at Paul Drake. "I don't get it," she said.

Mason said, "When I asked Minerva if she had the scar of an appendicitis operation, she promptly exhibited the precise spot where such a scar would have been.

"Now, if she hadn't read up on the location of such a scar, how would she have known the exact location to have exhibited? If you've had such an operation, you know where the scar is. If you haven't, you don't know, not unless you're a doctor, a nurse, or have read up on it."

"Now I get it," Della Street said, "but what was the scar she showed us when she first came to the office?"

"Tinted transparent tape and collodion," Mason said. "Remember her modesty? She backed into a corner away from the windows, bared herself for a moment, then overcome by modesty covered herself again. She didn't give any of us a really good look. Tinted tape and collodion can make an almost perfect surgical scar from a distance."

"But why in the world didn't you call the attention of the Court to what you had learned earlier in the trial?" Drake asked.

"Because if I had," Mason said, "Minerva Minden would have been convicted of the murder of Marvin Billings.

"After all, Dunleavey Jasper only needed to state that regardless of the lies he had told as to the first part of what had happened, that actually Minerva Minden had killed Marvin Billings.

"Remember also that Flossie Hendon was killed with Minerva's gun.

"I had to manipulate things just right so that the ending came in such a dramatic manner that Jasper would cave in all the way."

"But now the district attorney will prosecute Minerva on a hit-and-run charge," Drake said, "so I don't see that you've gained a thing."

"He won't prosecute her," Mason said.

"What makes you think he won't?"

"Because," Mason said, grinning, "she is going to make a voluntary appearance before the judge who had placed her on probation for her previous violations of the vehicle code. She is going to confess to her part in the hit-and-run accident and take her medicine."

"What will that medicine be?" Della Street asked. "Surely she's been punished enough because of this ordeal she's been through.''

''That,'' Mason said, ''is something we don't need to concern ourselves with. It's up to the judge. He may extend probation on this charge or he may revoke her probation and send her to jail. My own guess is he will find that the consequences of this last escapade of hers have resulted in subduing the madcap heiress of Montrose into a very penitent, humble young woman who now realizes she can't pit her personality, her wealth and her nylons against the majesty of the law.''

''You mean he will give her probation?'' Della Street asked.

''I think it's quite possible,'' Mason said. ''He will, of course, revoke her driving license for a long period and order her to make a generous settlement on the victim of the hit-and-run. Remember, she tried to confess to me on several occasions but I headed her off. I had to.''

''Why?'' Drake asked.

''Because,'' Mason said, ''I am an officer of the court. I didn't want her to confess to the hit-and-run crime until I had secured her release on this murder charge. I didn't want to have any official confirmation from her own lips of what I suspected to be the case until the murder charge had been disposed of.''

''But why did she take these elaborate precautions to fool us?'' Della Street asked. ''Why all the business of the blank cartridges at the airport?''

''Because,'' Mason said, ''she had found the ten thousand dollars in the glove compartment, had learned the car was a stolen one operated by crooks, and so she had to have Dorrie Ambler vanish into thin air in order to get the crooks off her own neck. Therefore, she put the ad in the paper, answered it herself, victimized the firm of detectives, and then called me *from the courthouse* as soon as the court hearing was over, saying she was at her apartment and that men were keeping her under surveillance and would we please come at once. Then Minerva hung up the telephone.

''You'll remember Drake's detective said she went to the phone booth right after the hearing. That's when she intended to have Dorrie disappear, leaving me very much concerned over the disappearance.

"It was a nice scheme. It *might* have worked the way she planned it. As it happened, however, at the time she was telephoning me, the crooks who had stolen the car and who had used the apartment on the lower floor as a base of operations were in the apartment searching for the ten thousand dollars. The detective caught them there and was shot by Dunleavey Jasper."

"Wouldn't it have been something," Della Street asked, "if you hadn't been able to bring things to such a dramatic conclusion that Dunleavey Jasper lost his head and confessed to what really happened? Good heavens, Minera Minden *might* have been convicted of her own murder!"

She thought for a moment, then asked, "How could Jasper have known all those facts, Chief?"

Mason grinned. "He didn't get the facts until later. Tragg's interview with us in the room that was bugged, and the subsequent story in the newspapers, gave him his chance to put one over on the police and Hamilton Burger. Jasper is smart. He desperately wanted immunity for his crimes — and of course he'd found Minerva's thirty-eight-caliber gun in the apartment at the Parkhurst. You can also bet that the police questioning gave him enough leads so he could build a pretty convincing story. Naturally the police were anxious to have all the details explained, and Jasper, having rented Apartment 805 and studied the tenant of 907, knew a lot of details he could use to make his story convincing. Because Hamilton Burger was so anxious to get something on me and to convict my client, he was an eager victim.

"Minerva Minden tells me she was out in the parking lot. The attendant thought she had been drinking and asked to see her driving license. She showed him the only license she had — the one in the name of Dorrie Ambler. The parking lot attendant remembered the

332

name, Ambler, and told Dunleavey Jasper he thought that was the name of the woman who had stolen his car. But Jasper, of course, didn't dare tell this to the police because it would ruin the story he was putting across, so he said on the stand he had located the car through underworld connections."

The phone rang. Della Street answered it, said, "Henrietta Hull wishes to know how much your fee is going to be."

Mason grinned. "Tell her it's one hundred and fifty thousand dollars and to make the check payable to the Children's Hospital. After all, I don't think Minerva should get off *too* easy."

The publishers hope that this Large Print Book has brought you pleasurable reading. Each title is designed to make the text as easy to see as possible. G. K. Hall Large Print Books are available from your library and your local bookstore. Or you can receive information on upcoming and current Large Print Books by mail and order directly from the publisher. Just send your name and address to:

G. K. Hall & Co.
70 Lincoln Street
Boston, Mass. 02111

F.